JUST ONE *Kiss*

Author of the Kiss Me Crazy Series

JAMI ROGERS

JUST ONE *Kiss*

Author of the Kiss Me Crazy Series

JAMI ROGERS

CHAPTER ONE

Kelsey

There's no point in making a plan because somehow it always manages to fall apart.

"I'm sorry, could you *please* repeat that?" I ask, even though I heard her loud and clear the first time.

Sara Connelly did *not* just tell me that in less than thirty days she'll be leaving on some "extended" vacation to finally travel the world—those are the exact words she used. Throw in the fact that she isn't sure when she'll be back, she isn't leaving me in charge of the bar while she's away, and someone else will be making my schedule, this doesn't look good for me. I can't decide whether to be relieved that she isn't adding to my newfound stress or hurt by her choice, seeing as a huge piece of my plan just went to shit.

"Any particular reason you made this choice?" I ask.

She just shakes her head.

After Sara graduated college at twenty-one—thanks to

early college classes she took while still in high school—her father gave her The Bar. Sara hated that name, so she had a reopening and renamed it The Black Alcove. Except everyone refers to it as the BA, which is fitting because it's been a year since she took over and the entire place is pretty badass.

That also means I've been the bar manager for the last year. I know my way around this place better than I do in the apartment Sara and I share. I can do anything she can do, and sometimes better. A new boss could and more than likely *will* ruin my already polished class schedule.

I stop slicing the lime in my hand, set the knife calmly on the bar top in front of me, and focus on her. Sara hasn't made eye contact with me once since she shared her announcement. *She's not telling me something.* She's sitting on one of the high-top stools at the other side of the bar, planning the next week's work schedule. She looks up from her papers and her long, blonde curls fall around her guilty face. Big, blue eyes look everywhere but at me before returning to the calendar lying in front of her. She clicks her pen twice before she says anything.

"Come on, Kelsey, this is your final semester of college. Do you really want to be running a bar and going to class?" She glances up. "Besides, we both know you hate working in general, and if I can't rely on you to show up on time to bartend the 3:00 p.m. shift, there's no way you can manage this place for a whole a year while I'm gone."

A whole year! I thought she didn't know how long she was going to be gone.

I let out a small huff, grabbing the knife and cutting into the green ball in front of me a bit more harshly than I should, all while cursing at how well she knows me. It's true. I hate being told what to do and when and where I need to be. I hate working. Correction—I hate working on a schedule someone else has made for me—even if it works around my classes—and rules are my enemy.

Yet here I am, about to graduate with a degree in accounting, which has nothing to with writing, my dream job. Writing would let me be anywhere at any time and be happy. Accounting will do nothing but give me a job where I'll have to work eight to five behind a desk. I'll probably work harder than I do as a bartender while making half the money. And that says something, because life as a bartender can be pretty intense work. What was I thinking?

Make Daddy proud. Maybe an accounting degree will get him to notice you. That's what I was thinking.

"I'm only late because I got lost in my studies." My voice is cheery and exaggerated.

"Ha, yeah okay, *studies*. I wasn't aware you were majoring in how to take the longest naps ever," she says, her voice dripping with sarcasm.

I give her my best sad face, bottom lip out and all. I can't help it when I fall asleep from a boring textbook. Hand me a romance novel or some suspense, and I'll pull an all-nighter.

"But the main reason I'm not leaving you in charge is because you stress easily. I don't want you becoming too overwhelmed this semester. It's your last one. Enjoy it."

That's sweet of her. But I still think she's holding back information.

The idea of new management terrifies me. I admit I need someone who can cut me some slack—college isn't as easy as some people make it look.

"Who is your replacement, and what if they fire me while

you're gone because they don't know how I work? They don't know me like you, and they won't 'let it slide' on account of the best friend rule."

It's quite simple: We always forgive each other no matter what and we don't judge each other or do anything that would cause the other to fail in life. Hence, if she fired me, I would fail in helping pay our rent.

"My cousin is coming to take over. I promise I already told him about you and that no matter what happens, he can't fire you." She shrugs, continuing to write out the schedule. Just like that. Problem solved. "Those weren't my exact words, but I run this place, not him. Technically he has to do what I say even if I'm not here. So you can stop having whatever huge mental freak out your having, because it doesn't look good on you."

I try not to smile. I was not having a *huge* freak out. Minor, possibly.

It's the first week of my final semester of college and everything should be going exactly the way I've written in my planner. A day shouldn't go by without having at least one item checked off. Even if it's as simple as watering the plants on Friday.

The main focus of my plan is the fact I'm housesitting for my parents for most of the semester, which means I'll have plenty of alone time to study and pass the last of my dreaded accounting classes. I still can't believe I left payroll accounting and tax income for the last semester. If I were smart, I would've taken them earlier. Scratch that, if I were *smart*, I would have enrolled in a degree for creative writing and taken a full credit load every semester to finish college earlier. But no, I didn't do that and now I'm graduating in the fall with a degree that means more to my father than me.

The next piece that makes my life so easy right now is working for Sara at The Black Alcove Bar. She's my best friend and my boss. It has its perks, such as my free-flowing schedule to work around homework and class. This bartending shift is defiantly a key player that's holding me and my perfected plan together. All my friends work here and it feels like home. We're a team that wants to succeed, and we do everything we can to help each other whether it's at work or not.

Another piece keeping me happy: the fact my cheating ex-boyfriend lives on the other side of town. And thank god for that because I throw up just a little in my mouth every time I lay eyes on him. All summer he's been finding reasons to "bump" into me. He feels like he needs to explain himself, but I understood the girl underneath him just fine. I'm ready for space to focus on me and what I want. To finish college and find a job writing before I find one in accounting.

The last and best part of my plans—there's still one more month to enjoy weekends sunbathing at the lake. In all honesty, I probably won't make it out there, but knowing I have the option is nice.

That's the plan. Plain and simple with no room for errors. Those details might not be the ones written down, but they are engraved inside my head and they aren't going anywhere. This final five months of college should be something I look forward to with a positive attitude. It's the time in my life when everything is finally coming together. I should be shouting and celebrating.

Unfortunately at this moment, I'm anything but positive.

"Well, maybe I can teach him to do what I say, too." We laugh at my joke even though a part of me really isn't joking. "Which cousin is it?" I ask, leaning my hip against the bar and glancing at the cooler behind me.

It should have been stocked last night, but Sara and Logan were closing. This is the third time in two weeks she's asked me to come in and help open after the two of them shut the place down. After her announcement, I'm starting to think it's her way of getting in some extra friend time. Either that, or she and Logan aren't actually working when they're together. I'm going with option B, but if I say that out loud, they will both deny it.

"Umm, Ethan," she says.

Ethan.

I freeze, resting my forearms against the counter.

"He was the cousin who used to stay with us over the summers. The same cousin you dumped a bucket of paint on when my dad was redoing the floor in this place." She pauses to look down. "I'm so glad he decided to go with the whole tie-dye floor thing. It gives this place some color."

I smirk. I only dumped the paint because Ethan was trying to remind me about our so-called "kiss." We got lucky when Sara's dad actually liked the mess I made. He went out and bought buckets of assorted colors, letting us kids go wild coating the cement floor. I aimed for Ethan with every bucket I touched.

"Anyway, his dad and my dad are brothers, so he's used to the whole owning your own business thing. Plus, he just got a business degree and wants to add this to his experience," she continues. "He's only a year older than us; you have to remember him."

Oh, I remember him. How could I forget? Still to this day no one knows what happened, not even Sara. I should have known geeks were the worst.

"You know he had that stupid mushroom haircut thing going on and glasses." Sara laughs, but then the giggles fade and she stares off at something behind me. I follow her gaze to find nothing important, and when I look back at her she's again focused on her papers. "That's the one problem with this plan. I haven't seen him in years. I hate to be shallow, but I can't have a nerd running this place. We have a reputation to uphold and he could ruin it."

She glances up. "Come on, Kelsey, you have to remember him."

Oh right, she's refreshing my memory. I give my head a slight nod as I pretend to remember.

"Yeah, he was the one who was always following us around. I bet we could still make him wait on us hand and foot." We both begin to laugh again but are quickly cut off.

"I don't think that's going to happen this time."

I jump at the deep voice that echoes inside the empty bar. In the doorway stands the most beautiful man I've ever seen. Tall, dark, and handsome doesn't even begin to describe him. *Is that ... Ethan?*

Sara hops off the stool with a giant smile on her face and quickly rushes to give him a hug. The veins that appear in his toned arms as he gives her a tight squeeze send a flutter through my entire stomach. *Holy crap, he's huge.* This is not the nerdy boy I remember. His body looks firm and sexy.

When Sara lets go of him, she turns to me. Her movement grabs my attention, snapping my eyes to hers before he can catch me checking him out.

"Kelsey, you remember Ethan," she says, and I can tell she's happy with her decision to leave him in charge. *Looks like her bar's reputation is going to survive.* "I was just telling Kelsey how you're going to take over for me while I'm gone," she says to Ethan. Although I don't think he heard her. His eyes are focused solely on me.

Ethan takes a step forward in his black shirt and blue jeans, and I watch him cautiously until he's standing in front of me. My fingers grip tighter onto the counter, trying to keep myself standing. He's even more gorgeous now than he was before.

His green eyes are bright against his short, black hair, and when he smiles, I know instantly that I don't stand a chance at holding my damn plan into place. *Not that I ever did.* He extends his hand to me, but I just stand there. I don't move. I don't do anything. Not even blink.

He lets out a deep chuckle, and my heart races so fast and loud, I swear he can hear it. "You haven't changed a bit." He raises an eyebrow, never taking his gaze off mine. "Still keeping quiet, I see."

I swallow and then break our eye contact. *Holy crap.* When I look up again, Ethan is glancing over to Sara, who's standing next to him, leaning against the counter.

"Is she this quiet with the customers too?" he jokes.

"No, she isn't," Sara says then looks at me with both eyebrows raised. She's trying to tell me something. She tilts her head toward Ethan and her eyes grow even bigger as they flicker toward Ethan and back to me.

I return my attention to Ethan and open my mouth.

Crap. What am I supposed to say? *Think, Kelsey, think. Either speak or close your mouth. You haven't spoken to him since that unfortunate summer. It was just one kiss, nothing to get worked up about. Don't embarrass yourself.*

I nod. "Hey," I say, wiggling my fingers and cringing at the pitch of my voice. "How's it going?"

Sara erupts into a fit of laughter I've never heard before, and I can feel my cheeks as they begin to blush. I look away the moment I feel the tears trying to fight their way forward. *Ohmygod! Ohmygod! Ohmygod!* So much for not embarrassing myself. How high did my voice seriously just go?

I stare at the countertop, pretending to be deeply distracted by a dent in the wood. I trace my finger over it and silently hope they'll leave soon, when Ethan's calming voice grabs my attention.

"Things are going good, just got to town. The wind here is annoying as hell, but I can get used to it," he says with a half grin. He winks at me then turns to Sara, who is staring at us with a satisfied smile on her face.

"Do you want go over my responsibilities out here or in your office?' he asks, getting right to the point of his visit.

"I'll meet you in there." She points her office.

"Cool," he says. "I'll see you around, Kelsey."

Ethan flashes a heart-stopping smile my way before he turns for Sara's office and disappears.

The moment he's out of sight, my breathing returns, and it feels like I just finished running a marathon.

"You are totally into him," Sara says, pointing behind her with her thumb and walking backward toward her office. "You were blushing a deep red just now. I can't believe I'm going to miss everything. Now, get out of here, and thanks again. I don't know why I get so on edge about the way Logan cleans at night. I promise one day I won't call you in to help last minute."

I don't respond to her while she laughs since my mind is still processing the fact Ethan is back and is going to be my new temporary boss.

After she closes the door, I let out a long breath before grabbing my purse from under the counter and marching out the door, straight to my car.

I round the corner from the bar and wave to Mrs. Mulligan, who's walking into the diner next to the BA. She waves back then stops to watch as I get closer to my car. She's nearing her eighties, which means she's starting to become very nosey. Something my mom warned me about—and she should know. As Mrs. Mulligan's neighbor, Mom has put up with more than a few surprise visits.

I pull the keys from my purse but pause mid-step when I see the large silver and shiny Toyota Tundra parked next to my tiny, white Ford Focus. The truck still has new plates and makes my car look like it's owned by a homeless person. God, even his truck is gorgeous.

I'm so totally screwed. I shouldn't be stunned into silence or struck in awe by Ethan or any other man. Men suck. Always have and always will.

Ethan

This is going to be one hell of a year.

I sit in one of the old torn chairs in front of Sara's desk, resting my hands behind my head as I wait for her. The chair squeaks when it leans back, and it goes far enough to make me think it's going to tip over. I sit up straight and pull my thoughts together.

I'm here to manage this place while Sara is away as a favor to my uncle, but mostly to get my father off my back. I'm not like him or my brothers. I can't manipulate people to get things I don't deserve. Like this bar, for example. If it weren't for the fact I'm sick of my father telling me how ungrateful I am and a pathetic man, I wouldn't be here secretly helping him sabotage his way into owning this place. Most normal guys my age would tell their dads to "fuck off," but not me. Family is important, and as shitty as they are some days, they're the only family I have. And that reason alone is why I'm here.

My mindset walking into this was "get in, get out in less than two weeks." Sara needs someone for almost a year, but the sooner my dad is happy, the sooner I don't have to listen to him anymore. But now, I might take a little longer. I wasn't expecting to walk in and find a certain slender and still beautiful brunette standing behind the counter.

Kelsey Brian.

One look from her and I forgot everything.

All she did was stand behind the counter, staring at me, and I already know there's no way I'm going to stop thinking about her. Hell, I don't think I ever have. Those big, golden eyes practically undressing me the minute I walked in the door. Her full, pink lips falling slightly apart as I walked closer. She smelled like Red Hots, the cinnamon candy, and my body had responded immediately.

I never could forget that girl. I wanted her so badly every summer I came here, to Wind Valley. That last time I was here, I had to beg my father to let me go. I had to have one last chance with her. When she found me during Sara's barbeque and pulled me to a hidden spot, I knew this was it. I was going to get exactly what I wanted. I was finally going to kiss her.

Then I ruined it.

My cell buzzes in my pocket. I pull it out to see a text from my father.

Dad: Don't let me down.

I read the message twice, remembering the last thing he said to me before I came here. *You better turn that heart to stone before you give the Connelly name a poor reputation.* My father's words are branded into my brain.

Fuck. As much as I hate it, I better repeat that every day. Kelsey's hot, but getting my dad off my back is more important right now than any woman.

Sara closes the door behind her and sits on the other side of her large desk. She doesn't say anything as she sorts through the papers in front of her, probably trying to find the one she needs. There are papers covering every inch of the wooden surface, and my need to always have things in order is trying to push its way out. I stand quickly and move to a bookshelf, picking up random pictures to keep my hands busy before I start to clean off her desk for her.

"Is everything okay?" she asks.

"Mmm hmm, everything's good." I glance down at her surroundings. *Fuck, this office is a mess.*

Sara smiles before finally clearing off a spot and setting a stack of papers on the open area. "These are for you. I need you to fill them out before we get started," she instructs, gesturing to the stack. "Thanks again for helping out. Our fathers couldn't have picked a better time to make up."

They haven't actually made up, but she doesn't need to know that. It is all an act my father put on to get me into this spot. Deep down, I know my father shouldn't be mad at my grandfather for leaving everything to Sara's father, but without my grandpa here to defend himself, my dad is taking it out on my uncle. And he's doing that by sending me here to find a few account numbers that he can use.

My grandfather's will said the bar belonged to my uncle. But there's also a clause that says if the day comes where money is misused in any form, the bar will then transfer to my father. Hence, my dad wants the account numbers to move money that isn't his into accounts that personally belong to my uncle.

"That will happen with stubborn old men," I say instead of the truth, returning to my seat across from her.

"What's it been … six or seven years since I last saw you?"

It's been seven, but if she can't remember, neither can I.

"Yeah, something like that."

Sara begins organizing her desk a little and I start filling out the paperwork. My mind is on autopilot as I fill in the blanks and I finish in record time. Once I'm done with that, I follow my cousin out of the office. The bar top that Kelsey was standing behind is a large L shape that takes up two walls, but there isn't anyone standing behind it now.

"It doesn't look like much during the day, but when it's

filled with people at night, it's my favorite place to be." Sara points to the corner. "We have a stage, but it's been weeks since there was a band on it. I'm working on a schedule for it now, but I'm waiting for a few phone calls." She spins, pointing to the corner by the front with the pool tables. "For now we use the jukebox for music."

I nod my head as she carries on about a couple more things.

This place is a lot cooler than I expected it to be. The space is in great shape and looks well taken care of. They don't have very many tables, but it works because they are more of an "enjoy the beer" place, not an "enjoy the food" place. The walls are blue, but you can hardly tell that with all the banners and neon signs. I'm actually excited that this is where I will hang out. It has a welcoming feel, and it's easy to see why business is good.

Sara's still talking when I glance at her. She moves around at ease with a smile. She doesn't notice me while she talks, so I survey the rest of the room.

It's obvious she and I are the only ones here now. Good. I need to ask her if she needs anything else from me because I have an appointment with the Realtor to pick up the keys for the house I'm leasing. It takes me a minute to realize Sara isn't talking anymore. She's watching me when it clicks.

"What's with the smile?" I ask.

She instantly blushes and her posture straightens.

"What smile?"

"The one on your face that screams, 'I'm up to something.' You wore that smile a lot when we were kids. I know it better than you think."

"I'm not up to anything, Ethan," she says with a straight

face then walks behind the bar. Slowly that sneaky smile reappears, and I can tell she's trying to hide it. For whatever reason, she doesn't want to tell me and that's fine. I'm not here to build a relationship. Not with her anyway.

"Thanks again for hiring me."

"Oh yeah, no problem. It was you or Kelsey, and, well …" She looks up again, still smiling. "She needs a little help with the whole staying-on-schedule thing. I think hiring someone else to be her manager might motivate her to take that next step."

Ahhh. I'm catching on now. I don't think having a different manager is going to motivate her. It's *who* her new manager is that will motive her. Women—they're not as sneaky as they think they are. But heck, I'll play along. If it means more time with Kelsey, I'll do whatever my cousin wants me to.

Whoa.

Where did that come from? More time with Kelsey is the last thing I need.

"Come back tomorrow at three. You can follow one of the bartenders around for a bit to get the flow of things," Sara says before a tall man and a woman with firecracker-red hair wearing black shirts with the bar's logo on them approach from a back room. The guy unlocks the front door and a gray-haired couple walk in. The elderly love arriving right at opening. I assume these two will be the only customers for at least another hour.

I nod on my way out, but Sara greets the old couple. She shares a laugh with them and even gives them each a polite hug. She looks happy here, and for a minute I feel guilty. I'm going to be the bad guy and help take it from her.

Right before I step through the exit, I hear her call my name. I turn to see her coming toward me with a smile. She wraps her arms around me, giving me a tight hug then steps away.

Yep, I'm the bad guy already.

CHAPTER TWO

Kelsey

For the next five months, my parents will be touring France, Italy, and Germany. They've left me in charge of everything they own, and this is night one. I've already managed to lock myself out. *Go me.*

"You're not seriously going to break in, are you?" Sara asks through the phone.

"What choice do I have, Sara? All my stuff is in their house, and my dad was very clear on his rules. Make sure the sprinkler system comes on each morning till the end of August, dust everything, cleaning includes bathrooms, and don't drive the cars. That's just the small list. For all I know, he could have a camera set up to make sure I do as he instructed."

Without a key, breaking in is the only way to go. He didn't say don't break anything or break *into* anything, but those are probably basic rules. Still, he never actually said it.

"This sucks. I'm gone in less than four weeks, and you're

not even going to be staying in our apartment until I leave. You could come home and crash here for just one more night. Then we can call the locksmith in the morning."

I shake my head, refusing her offer even though she can't see me. Sara's suggestion is good, but it's not going to work. Not right now. Not when my computer is inside this house and my fingers are itching to get some writing in before I go to bed.

I'm sitting alone in my car in my parents' driveway. It's in a new neighborhood just east of town, and they picked a fully beige house. I call it "The Palace of Beige." Everything is that boring ass color—the house, the trim, the doors. Everything. It has a three-floor layout with five bedrooms, each with their own bath; a movie room; and a four-car garage. They have two kids who no longer live at home and four cars. What a waste of money.

"That defeats the whole purpose of housesitting, Sara." I move my cellphone to my left ear and hold it in place with my shoulder as I turn off my car. The wind is intense tonight, and my car moves in a wave-like motion with each gust. Thankfully, it stopped raining so I can see a little better, but it's almost midnight and everything is pitch black. Add the fact I forgot to leave the front porch light on and the fact the subdivision has a lot of houses still in the building phase, and it makes this whole situation creepy. I've watched too many movies of what can go wrong in a construction zone.

"Okay, so what are you going to do? Throw a rock through the window, crawl inside, and then claim someone broke in while *you* were watching their house? I guarantee they won't give you the money they offered. In fact, I bet they would make you replace it with your own cash. You should totally rethink whatever plan you have devised in your head."

Lose out on five grand for five months of housesitting? Easiest money ever. I need it so I can start a career in self-publishing. I could buy a new window and still come out ahead.

"It's my only option. I'll call you when I'm inside."

Sara's voice raises a few pitches, but I end the call before I can hear what she says. I know she's right that I should just wait till tomorrow, but writing is way more important than whatever window I'm about to bust.

I open my car door only to have it blown shut by the strong August wind the moment my left leg is out. *Ouch!* Only this stupid Wyoming wind would stick around for every day of the year. I push the door off my leg and jump out of the car in a hurry to avoid the same mistake. The wind again slams the door shut at the same time I firmly plant my feet into the ground to keep from blowing away. My long, brown hair is whooshing in all directions and it's a battle between Mother Nature and my hand to keep it away from my eyes long enough to walk to the house.

Each step is like pulling a semi-truck behind me. It's like I'm not even moving. Thank goodness I went with blue jeans and a black hoodie tonight. Trying to keep a dress or skirt down in this mess would be pointless.

I finally make it to the front porch, pulling my smartphone from my back pocket to turn on the flashlight. I shine the light around the windows and over the deck in search of a hide-a-key. When I come up short, I catch sight of a curtain blowing freely inside the house. *Yes!* There must be a window open. I hold the flashlight against the window to pinpoint my next destination. Perfect, I should be able to climb through from the back porch.

I leap off the front steps, not making much distance when the wind pushes me backward. The ball of my foot catches the last step and I fall. I hit the steps just perfectly to pinch the skin on the back of my thigh, and a small scream passes my lips as I roll on the ground, grabbing the tender area and trying not to cry.

You had to remember one thing, Kelsey. The key. This whole mess could have been avoided had you remembered the key.

After allowing myself a minute to scold myself, I push off the ground and head for the back porch. I walk around to the left side of the house and come to a complete, firm stop, not giving the wind a chance to blow me down. What the—when did they do this? A fence. A stupid tall, white, keep-the-burglar-out-of-my-yard wooden fence. Right where I need to be. Okay. I get it. Lesson learned. I will never forget the key, or any key for that matter, ever again.

I force my way to the fence and sigh with relief when my fingers can reach the top. If I jump just a little, I should be able to pull myself over. Finally, someone is on my side.

I extend my arms as straight as I can get them, but they don't get a good enough grip on the top of the fence when I jump. A few more tries later, it's still not enough. I bend at the knee and swing my arms behind to give myself the extra oomph I need. The sound of an empty dumpster hitting the pavement startles me, and I quickly turn around.

"Who's there?" I call out. I can't see anything; it's too dark. It was probably just a cat or the wind. Either way, that's all the motivation I need to get over this fence. This time my effort is just good enough to haul myself over. Or—maybe not. My arms are stuck mid-pull, ready to give out. *I should really start working out*. This is just stupid. As I hang on the fence, I hear the sound of footsteps on the grass behind me. Instantly I have the strength I need and I pull myself halfway up. All I need to do it swing my legs over and it's done.

Suddenly, my body goes stiff and I'm pretty sure I've stopped breathing.

Someone is touching me.

Ethan

After finding every excuse I could to get out of dinner with my cousin—the less time with Kelsey around me, the better—all I wanted to do was get some sleep. Instead, I'm wide awake and irritated with my new neighbors.

I woke up when I heard a car door slamming and a light scream minutes after. This is not the way my first night in my first home should go. I'm no pansy, but it's a good thing I own guns because if this shit goes down every night, then I damn sure better stay alert. I'll be ready for whoever wants to break into my house.

I drag myself out of bed and down the stairs to look out the front window. There's some chick across the street rolling around on the ground in front of my neighbor's house. When she shifts, I can see that she has a flashlight in her hand. This is not normal behavior for most people.

I watch as she pushes herself up and rounds the house, coming to a stop. I can't see her face because the wind is out of control, blowing her hair in all directions, and right before she turns toward my house, she pulls the hood of her sweatshirt over her head. She stands there for a minute, shoulders slumped.

Just when I think this bizarre mini-event is over the girl marches up to the fence, reaches her hand high, and then starts jumping. I don't know the people in my neighborhood yet, but this isn't a good sign.

I don't waste any time as I slip my shoes on and run out the door. I'm wearing only a pair of black gym shorts, and this wind feels like ice against my skin. My goal is to sneak up on her, but after a huge gust of wind comes out of nowhere, I lose balance and bump into the dumpster. Sneaking is no longer an option. I run straight for the intruder and get there just in time.

She is half over the fence, dangling her upper body on one side and her legs on the other. My side. The legs also come with a very nice ass that's hard to miss.

I wrap my hands around her ankle and pull her toward me. There's no way I am letting her over this fence. Nice ass or not.

The eardrum-busting scream that comes out of her mouth is not what I'm expecting. I start to shake my head to get the ringing to stop at the same time she starts yelling. I can't hear her very well because my ears are still recovering.

"Let me go!" she demands.

"No way! I'm not letting you over this fence," I shout back.

Her body goes stiff and the screaming stops. I think I hear her whisper the word "no," but I'm not sure. If she's trying to talk me into letting her go, it's not working. I use this moment to tug on her legs, attempting to pull her back over. Instantly she starts resisting, giving it her all as she tries to wiggle her way out of my grip.

"Just jump back down and we …"

Fuck!

The stinging pain of her foot making solid contact with my face distracts me and I lose my balance, again. My hand loosens its grip, and as I stumble backward, I grab her ankle to keep myself from falling. It doesn't work and we both fall to the ground.

I grunt when she lands on top of my stomach, making it hard to breathe. She pulls herself together, quickly rolling off me and scrambling to her feet, but I'm faster. I grab her foot and yank her back until she is under me. With my legs on either side of her, my arms are straight as I hold her arms tightly against her sides to keep her pinned to the ground. She wiggles hard trying to escape.

"Don't touch me!" she hollers and continues to attempt yanking her arms out of my grip while trying to sit up.

"Yeah, no, that's not going to happen. You can't just go breaking into someone's house and get away with it."

Her body goes lifeless under my hands and she takes a sharp breath. When she opens her eyes to face me, I almost let go. The wind has blown her hair out of her face, giving me a perfect view of bright, gold eyes piercing me with a heated glare. Her creamy white skin glows in the darkness, rendering me speechless.

Kelsey.

For a moment neither of us says anything. Maybe she wasn't breaking in after all. Someone this beautiful can't be that crazy. Can she? Sara definitely would have told me if her best friend has a few screws loose.

The stunned moment is interrupted when I hear the sound of sirens approaching. *Just awesome.* Someone called the cops. Kelsey uses the distraction and shoves me off of her, quickly rising to her feet.

"You called the police on me? Seriously? This night just keeps getting better," she snaps.

"I didn't call the cops. I had it handled," I spit back at her.

She takes a step toward me, dramatically placing her hands on her hips.

"Oh you had IT handled, huh?" Her eyes roam over my face. Where is the quiet, innocent girl I saw earlier today? I guess the silent streak is over. As her eyes meet mine, they look so cold I can't help but take a step back. "Yeah," she says with a laugh, "your face is covered in blood. You had IT handled real well."

Blood. Really?

I reach up to my face and sure enough, when I touch my nose, there's blood everywhere.

"You kicked me in the face," I growl, defending myself.

"You deserved it," she says, jabbing her finger into my chest.

As the sirens get louder, she begins to look around frantically, turning to sprint away only to be cut off when a police car pulls up in front of the house.

The cop gets out of the car, walks to the front of his vehicle, and stops. He's tall and in better shape than I would think a cop his age should be. Definitely not someone I want to mess with, and that says something since I work out every day.

The cop stands with his hands on his hips and begins to shake his head.

"Kelsey Brian," he says, and a smile appears on his face. "It's been too long since I last saw you."

As if the night weren't weird already, the fact Kelsey is on a first-name basis with a cop just made everything about her more interesting.

Kelsey

Never say things could be worse. The moment you think it, it happens.

Like right now, my cheating ex-boyfriend's father, who also happens to be a cop, is standing in front of me, waiting to arrest me no doubt.

"Officer Maron." I roll my eyes and cross my arms. I shouldn't be rude, but this cannot be happening right now. I want to get inside my car and leave this awful situation. It's cold out, and now I'm going to have to suffer this stupid wind even longer. My urge to write is officially gone.

He nails me with his judgmental glare, and I look everywhere but directly at him. His presence is pushing all the wrong buttons as he stands there looking well groomed with his ocean-clear blue eyes, blonde hair, and sharp facial features that are an exact match to his son's. *Makes me sick.*

The story of Tyler and me went way beyond any clichéd story of walking in on your boyfriend and catching him cheating red-handed. He was on the couch, lying naked on top of someone. I heard a moan, and my gasping caught their attention. That's when another chick—also naked—came walking out of our bathroom, asking Tyler where his other box of condoms was because they were all out.

"Um, sir?" Ethan speaks up somewhere behind me. I don't move as my eyes narrow and peek sideways until I can see him. *He's still here.* I can't tell if I'm excited or mad that the dark- haired god who arrived earlier today is back in the middle of the night. Attacking me like some crazed lunatic.

I watch as Ethan runs a hand through his hair and lets out a breath. What's he doing here anyway? And where is his shirt? I take a quick glance and swallow hard. *Never mind.* The shirt can stay gone.

His eyes don't look cold anymore—just the opposite, almost as if he feels sorry for me. How can someone show so many emotions with just their eyes? They have that added extra sparkle to them that you only read about in books. I smile at him and his face quickly falls to confusion.

Wait.

I'm pissed at this guy. I'm still standing here only because of him. I give Ethan another dirty look that quickly fades when he starts to laugh. *Damn it.* If I don't get my thoughts in check, he will never take me seriously at work.

"Young man, it's probably best you head home. This doesn't concern you," Mr. Maron says.

He can't be serious.

"It sure as hell concerns him." I shift my body and point at the culprit. "He attacked me while I was trying to get inside. You should be arresting him, not sending him home."

"Attack you? I was saving these people—" Ethan says, pointing to The Palace of Beige"—the hassle of dealing with a robbery when they get home."

Mr. Maron steps off the road and into the grass to approach us. He releases a small laugh.

"What happened here? Who robbed who?" he asks, confused.

"He attack—"

"She was break—"

Oh, Ethan did not just cut me off. I glare at him and practically growl when Mr. Maron cuts us both off.

"Whoa now," he says and holds his arms out at his sides, warning us to keep our distance. Probably a good idea at this point, since I'm so angry I'm sure they can see the flames shooting from my eyes. Mr. Maron looks at me. "Kelsey, why are you here?"

Dang right, he should ask me first.

"I'm housesitting and forgot my key. I left the back window open and was making my way to it when this guy attacked me." I cross my arms again and with a smirk I give Ethan a look that tells him this is over. He shouldn't even try to argue his way out of it. Ethan raises an eyebrow that clearly accepts the challenge. My smirk vanishes and my breathing picks up.

Mr. Maron nods his head, pulling a small notebook from his back pocket and removing the pen from the collar of his shirt.

"Alright, what's your name, son, and why are you here?" His voice sounds sterner this time.

"Ethan Connelly, and I live in that house." He sounds annoyed as he points to the dark green, not beige, house directly across the street. *He lives there?* "Some weird noises woke me up, and when I looked out the window, I saw this chick trying to climb this fence. I assumed she was breaking in."

First I'm an *it* and now I'm some *chick*?

I give a sarcastic laugh and roll my eyes. My name must have just slipped his mind.

Mr. Maron shakes his head, releasing an aggravated breath.

"Next time, call the police. You can go home now. I can handle things from here."

The thought of being left alone with my ex's father worries me. He will ask questions and I'll stay quiet, just like I always do. We were practically family, and now it hurts too much to talk to him. For a brief moment I consider asking Ethan to stay. I open my mouth but he takes a step toward his house, giving me a winning grin. My body shudders. Cocky guys are so unattractive. Never mind that idea; I don't need him. At the same time Ethan steps off the sidewalk, I turn for my car.

"Wait a minute, Kelsey. We still need to talk."

Of course we do. Things can never be easy. My shoulders slump forward as I impatiently wait for a man who was practically my father-in-law to continue.

"It's been awhile since I saw you last." He pauses. "You know you're always welcome in our home, Kelsey. If you ever want or need to talk … Emily and I are always here." His voice is so gentle, and I know he means every word.

I take a deep breath, trying to calm myself before the waterworks start. For three years this man was more of a father to me than my own. Yes, it's wrong of me to shut them out, but things are different now and I don't want to be the crazy ex-girlfriend who still hangs out with her ex-boyfriend's family. It doesn't matter that Tyler is the one who invites me over half the time. Says he still wants to be friends because I am and will always be his best friend, but I don't think I'm strong enough for that. I can't trust myself to look at him and not miss what we had. What I had. A best friend I could tell anything to, who I thought I could trust to always be honest.

"I'm fine," I say, forcing the words out of my mouth. It's been long enough I shouldn't let it affect me anymore.

Mr. Maron doesn't say anything as he comes up behind me. He gives me a quick shoulder hug and then continues to the porch. He stops at the top of the steps, looking around. If he can find the hide-a-key for me, maybe I'll talk.

I watch as he shines his flashlight around—a real one, searching every crack, corner, and flowerpot. At the door, he reaches for the knob, turns it slowly, and the door opens. My mouth drops open when he looks back at me with an "are you kidding me?" look that I choose not to respond to. I march right past him and shut the door once I'm inside. Thank goodness he didn't find the hide-a-key.

CHAPTER THREE

Kelsey

The clock next to my bed finally hits 7:00 a.m. I toss the covers and slowly pull myself from the guest room's king-size bed. Sleeping was difficult last night. I dozed off fast, but my mind wasted no time dreaming of Ethan and the way he looked in just a pair of shorts. That's a lie. My mind dreamt more of what his body looked like *without* those shorts. His entire body looked so firm that if I ever bumped into him, I might break something. I woke up after an hour, sweating and blushing at how real the dream felt. Then, I fell back to sleep and the process repeated itself over and over.

I pull a pair of sweats over my black Spandex, grab a hoodie, and lace my shoes. Running is the best way for me to gain a clear mind, and god knows I need to clear the shit out of it right now. I tie my hair up and don't waste any time getting out the door. Since Ethan is successfully taking up every available inch of headspace, today's run won't be anything short of an hour.

* * *

I return to my parents' house, shedding myself of my hoodie and sweats, leaving myself in only my Spandex and a sports bra to cool down. I stroll into the kitchen to fix myself a cup of coffee and a quick breakfast. Every Tuesday and Thursday I have my payroll class at nine in the morning and a creative writing class at one. I couldn't care less about payroll, but I want to be 100 percent focused on creative writing.

I still have my headphones on as I pour myself a cup of coffee, so when my cellphone rings, it changes the song blaring music into my ears. I pull on the cord like my headphones are on fire.

"Hello," I greet, quickly holding my phone a tiny way from my ears until they've stopped buzzing.

"Kelsey, what took you so long to answer and why do you sound out of breath? Is everything okay with the house?"

It should come as a surprise that my father would relate my shortness of breath to the house, not my life being in danger, but it doesn't. I'm almost positive my father never wanted a daughter. Once I got my first bra, he never attempted to have a relationship with me, and he's always favored my little brother. They are so close it's disgusting. Sometimes I forget he's our father and not one of my brother's immature friends.

It still stuns me that my father is even letting me housesit for them. He could have hired someone, but my father trusts no one. In fact, I'm sure I wasn't his first pick and my mother had to convince him to let me do this. Then again, my brother doesn't live in Wind Valley, so Dad doesn't really have an option.

"Hello, Kelsey, are you there?"

"Yes, I am, sorry. I went for a run and just got back," *No worries, Dad, your precious house is just fine.*

"Good. You haven't had any problems, have you? Mrs. Mulligan next door called your mother last night and said there was a disturbance."

I roll my eyes and prop my hip against the marble counter to stare out the back kitchen window at Mrs. Mulligan's small blue and white house. She's outside in her gardening clothes but peeking over her back fence right into my parents' kitchen. She smiles and waves. I will have to talk to her later.

"It was nothing, Dad, I promise." I look at my feet and take a deep breath. "Is Mom there?" I ask and he grunts through the phone. He doesn't answer me, but soon enough my mother's calming voice is on the line. My parents are the perfect example of opposites attract.

"Hi, honey," she greets me in her soft tone, and my body relaxes completely. "How is your morning going? Have you had any classes yet?"

"My first one is today at ..." I walk over to the table and open my backpack, which is sitting on one of the chairs, and pull out my schedule. I know it by heart, but I feel the need to read it one more time, and I glance at the clock and then do a double take. My first class starts in twenty minutes! My run couldn't have been *that* long.

"I'm sorry, Mom, I have to go. I'm running late. I love you, have fun!" I tell her and hang up the phone. I swing my backpack over my shoulder and grab my keys off the table before running out the door.

. . .

Ethan

Normally, I don't wake up until I hear my alarm beeping, but today is different. Today, the unfortunate sound of someone's car straining to start wakes me. By the sounds of it, I won't be falling back to sleep anytime soon. Any other day I would be fine with it, but I'm already in a bad mood from a sleepless night. Mainly because I couldn't stop thinking about Kelsey. The cop knew her by name, which is never a good sign and it makes me wonder what she's been up to. And partially because my face feels like it was hit by a bus and it won't stop throbbing.

My phone rings at the same time I roll off my bed. I grab it off the nightstand and the name Max Connelly is flashing across the screen. My father.

"Hello," I answer as I wander into the bathroom. I tried to clean up the bloody mess on my face as best I could before I went to bed, but the pain then was a good sign it's not going to look good now. When I spot my reflection in the mirror, I'm not the least bit surprised. She got me good. My nose is swollen, as are the two black eyes on either side.

"How did the first day go?" my father asks, getting right to business.

"It was brief, but tonight one of the bartenders is going to train me." There's no point in making small talk with Max Connelly. The man is all business. By participating in this plan of his, I've got more attention from him in the last two weeks than I have since I was born.

"Training?" He laughs. "Need I remind you that our family owns this bar, Ethan? If you do not feel you're capable of doing what I've asked from you, I will replace you with one of your brothers who can." His voice is firm and I know he will keep his word if I fail.

"I will do exactly what I need to get this done, sir. You have my word," I tell him as I run a small towel under warm water and gently wipe away the dried blood.

"Good. I'll be expecting a twenty-four hour update until I'm confident with leaving you there. Best of luck today, son," he says and the line goes dead. What a way to start my day. And I know for a fact he isn't really wishing me luck.

My head drops forward when I hear the persistent noise of the still-dead car that is inexorable from my bathroom window. Doesn't this person get the hint? *Your car isn't going to start, so just give up already.*

I don't want to turn into that nosy neighbor, but damn, this neighborhood is noisy. I toss the towel into the sink, and once again head down the stairs to see who's making such a racket.

I open the blinds completely this time. The weather is clear, the sky is blue, and the sun is shining.

I hear the noise again and quickly find the source. I close my eyes and take a deep breath. *Kelsey.*

I don't bother pulling on a pair of shoes this time. It will only take me a couple seconds to offer my help. Nothing I can't do in a pair of gym shorts. I jog lightly across the street and slow to walk up the driver's side of her car. I notice her phone sitting on the ground by her door and kneel down to pick it up. Unfortunately for me, Kelsey chooses this exact moment to get out of her car. By the force of the metal against my forehead, it's obvious she is taking her frustration out on the door.

"Oh my god!" she gasps, covering her mouth with her hand. "I'm so sorry I didn't see you there."

I stand, slowly extending my hand that holds her phone. I'm rubbing my head with my other hand when she comes into view clearly. And fuck. What is she wearing? Or better yet—what isn't she wearing? Kelsey's standing less than an arm's length away from me in nothing but a tiny pair of black shorts and a sports bra. My hand falls quickly as I shift my stance. These shorts don't leave much to the imagination.

Still covering her mouth, Kelsey's eyes grow wider and start to glaze over. She moves her hand from her mouth and reaches toward me but quickly pulls back.

"I'm so … so … I hope you're okay." She takes a deep breath then looks away.

"I'm fine." It comes out a bit more harsh than planned. But if I didn't know any better, I'd think this girl is slowly trying to kill me. *It's always the good-looking ones, isn't it?*

Kelsey's look of remorse quickly fades, turning into the same heated glare from last night. She crosses her arms and cocks her head.

"Is there a reason you're standing in my driveway?"

Her driveway? I thought she was housesitting.

"I came over here to offer you my assistance." I nod toward her car. "It sounds like you need help starting your car. And for as much as I would love to watch you stand out here half naked, you're disturbing the whole neighborhood. I'll go get my truck and give you a jump." I take a step around her.

I honestly think explaining to her why I'm here will help her not look so panicked, but instead, I get a dramatic gasp before she takes off to hide inside. I shake my head as I wander back across the street for some jumper cables. This is going to be one hard woman to figure out.

CHAPTER FOUR

Kelsey

How humiliating. I was just standing there, having a normal conversation while practically naked. Naked in front of Ethan of all people. I'd been so concerned about getting to class on time, I didn't even consider what I'm wearing. And he didn't have much on either, just that same damn pair of black mesh shorts I'd dreamed about. I could barely focus with his solid body and six pack abs just staring at me.

This is karma for lying to Sara to get out of dinner last night. I should have just gone to the apartment. All I wanted was to avoid seeing Ethan, which didn't happen anyway. Now, I've seen him twice in less than twenty-four hours, and I've physically left the guy beaten and bruised. My day couldn't get any worse. I should probably just skip school and call in to work before I can do any more damage.

I won't be able to run and hide at the BA. Worse yet, I could spend the whole evening daydreaming by just looking at his face, bruises and all.

I stand with my back against the front door, tapping my head against it, trying to forget what just happened. I swear if I pull one more embarrassing stunt in front of him, I'll die. Sara will likely de-friend me, and I'll lose my job. I mean, come on, I'm a hazard when it comes to Ethan. Starting from the day he kissed me while he had a girlfriend.

I pull my purse in front of me and dig around for my phone like my life depends on it. When it dawns on me that my phone is already in my hand, I quickly dial Sara's number. She picks up after two rings.

"Oh perfect timing," she says into the phone. "I was just about to text you. I'm calling a last-minute mandatory meeting before we open today."

Oh great. Even more time to spend with Ethan. My heart beats faster.

"So do you think you can make it early enough for the meeting?"

"Yeah I think so. I'll stop by this afternoon to help get things ready. Do you want anything from the Coffee Shack? If I'm going in early, I'm going to need coffee."

Sara tells me her order, and after we hang up I run upstairs to shower. If I'm going to make any class today, it will be creative writing. If I time it right, I might even be early for work.

It's only after I've stepped out the door an hour later that I remember my car is dead. I glance across the street. Ethan's truck is gone. *Damn.* Now what? Asking Mrs. Mulligan is not even an option.

There's a note under one of my wipers. I look around once more, then grab the white piece of paper and unfold it.

. . .

Kelsey,

I went ahead and gave your car a jump before I left. See you at the meeting.

Ethan

P.S. Please don't leave your car unlocked again. People are crazy.

Ethan

Relief floods me and I can't stop the grin on my face as I turn the key. The engine starts right up. After everything I have done to him, he still helped me. I should probably do something nice for him as a thank you. Maybe I'll get him a coffee too. After all, I did interfere with his sleep last night.

Ethan

I debated whether or not to help Kelsey with her car after she stormed off, but then I remembered the way her cheeks turned that soft shade of pink right after I told her she should be wearing more clothes. I probably caught her off guard and somehow embarrassed her. Although, there was nothing for her to be embarrassed about. She looks amazing. I'm more upset with the fact anyone could see her and I don't want them to.

I lock the door behind me and pull my phone out of my pocket as I head to my truck. Logan Parker is one of the few people I know in this town other than my cousin and a couple other guys I used to hang out with over the summer. I've kept in touch more with Logan than my own family. I dial his number and climb inside my truck

"Ethan, man, what's up?" Logan answers after the third ring.

"Not much—just heading out. Can you meet up?" It's in my best interest that I try to make things look as normal as possible. Those are my father's words, not mine. It won't be hard with Logan. He really is a friend.

"Meet up? You back in town or what?" Logan asks.

"Yeah, I'm helping Sara with the bar while she's gone."

"What? Sara's leaving?" He sounds surprised. She must not have told anyone yet. That's probably why she called this unexpected meeting today. He continues before I can reply. "Yeah, okay, do you want to meet at the old diner between the bar and that coffee place downtown?"

Almost everything in Wind Valley can be found in what the locals call "downtown." It's four blocks in the middle of town and in the perfect shape of a box, with a park in the center. Three of the blocks have about ten businesses apiece and the other block is all apartment buildings. I know Sara lives in one of them. It makes sense since the BA is downtown.

"Yeah, sounds good, man—in an hour?"

"No, I have class till two today. How about around two-thirty?" he suggests.

I tell him two-thirty is good, and after we hang up, I start my truck. I glance over at Kelsey's house, or, rather, the one she's housesitting for. The thought of her brings a smile to my lips. She's a feisty one and I like it. I like knowing she's living there, near me. A friendship is a possibility between us, but who am I kidding? I could never just be her friend.

If I weren't so focused on being on good terms with my father, maybe Kelsey and I would have a real shot at something. But no, I've waited twenty-two years for my father to accept me. I can't back out now.

The image of Kelsey in Spandex flashes in my eyes. Until I have those account numbers, we'll be spending a lot of time together. Can we honestly work together without me wanting to put my hands all over her? I shake my head as I shift into gear and pull away.

My bet right now is no.

CHAPTER FIVE

Kelsey

It takes me so long to find a parking space on campus that I'm now going to be late for my writing class. *Big surprise.* I seriously consider parking at the BA since the campus is only a few blocks away, but even then, it would add three blocks of running.

I sprint up the steps and through the double doors of the Littman Building. It's the one and only building I have never been in. I stop just inside the doors, looking at the directory on the wall. Great. My destination is at the other end of the building. I walk briskly down the hallway, not making eye contact with anyone to avoid any distractions. I would speed up, but the "no running in the halls" rule has stuck with me my whole life. Probably the one and only rule, too.

When I finally reach the classroom, the door is closed. I open it slowly, not wanting to draw attention to myself, but the door creaks and everyone turns in their seats. My body goes stiff as I pause in the doorway, taking in all the unfamiliar faces. Someone raises their hand—Logan, one of the other bartenders at the BA and a close friend of mine, is waving at me.

I quietly make my way over to the right side of the room where he is sitting and slide into the seat next to him. Just as I set my backpack on the on the floor, a short, bald man wearing a navy-blue suit and carrying a worn-out, brown briefcase walks into the classroom, letting the door slam closed behind him.

I jump in my seat and the class falls silent.

"The scariest moment is always just before you start," the man I assume is the professor says, projecting his raspy voice. "Author Stephen King said this: how many of you would agree?" He scans the room. One by one, students raise their hand, me included. He remains quiet until everyone in the class has a hand in the air.

"I agree as well, although I feel this fits for any moment in life, not just writing. Now, we have started class and you can all relax—the scary part is over." Everyone lets out a laugh as he steps around the square table that was behind him and unzips his bag.

"My name is Professor Frank. You may call me Frank during the class hour. Here is the class syllabus for the semester." He hands a stack to a redheaded boy in the front row, who takes one and passes the rest. "Please read it over and let me know if you have any questions. I will say this once and that's it. I am not your mother or your father. I will not scold you for not doing your work, nor will I scold you for not showing up to my class. I will not deduct points for missing class, but I do suggest you make a friend to collect any handouts because I do not store the extra copies for you to get at a later date. But like most teachers, I do hope you show up to every class I teach."

The next hour flies by, but I'm still disappointed when class ends. I lift my bag over my shoulder.

"Before I forget," the professor says as students begin their exit, "during this semester, our local newspaper will be searching for a new columnist to be chosen in contest form from the students participating in my classes. You do not have to be an English major to enter. The entry forms are here on the corner of my desk."

I don't think twice before I take one of papers he offers, quickly skimming the rules. Two-hundred-fifty-word column of your choice. Top five chosen to attend a formal dinner. Winner signs two-year contract with full salary.

Satisfied, I tuck the form into my notebook and follow Logan out of building. This is the class I was looking forward to the most, so I was hoping for our first assignment. I'm probably his only student who wants homework on the first day, and my other professors should not get this idea confused with their classes. I just want to write. Learning about this contest will fill that void for now.

"Thank god he didn't give us homework on the first day. I suck at writing," Logan shares with me as we walk to my car.

"Then why did you take this class?" I ask, trying not to laugh. What kind of person doesn't like to write?

"I needed one more elective and Sara told me you'd be enrolled in this one. I figured it wouldn't hurt to have a least one class where I know someone."

"Aww, Logan … you think we're friends?" I joke as we reach my car.

"Ha, funny, Kels," he says walking backward with a smile "See you at the meeting."

"Wait … do you need a ride?" Logan lives in the building next to Sara and me. It's close to the college, so he usually walks, but I am hoping today is different. I need an extra pair of hands when I pick up coffee for Sara, Ethan, and I.

"Nope, got plans," he shouts before turning around and heading downtown toward his apartment.

I'll be fine without him. I'm a bartender for crying out loud—I know how to successfully carry three drinks at once. Piece of cake.

Ethan

I needed to do a few things before meeting up with Logan, and my last stop is close enough to the diner I can walk. We'll probably visit only for an hour or less before the BA meeting starts, and I need to think about what I'm going to say if he asks why I'm back in town. The simple "helping out the family" might work, but I haven't been back in a while and Sara and Logan aren't strangers. He more than likely knows our families have been feuding for years. It never came up with us, but that doesn't mean he doesn't know.

I stop at the corner and wait for the little walk man to show up on the light. I'm going to be early to the diner, but I don't mind. A few minutes of silence alone never hurt anyone. It'll give me just enough time to get Kelsey and that tiny outfit she was wearing this morning off my mind before Logan shows up.

I'd hoped by the time I'd signed up for a gym membership and gone grocery shopping, she would be off my mind. It was going good until I passed an aisle with a pair of ear plugs hanging on the end. Then all I thought about was last night.

Maybe if I stop trying to avoid her, I won't be so interested when I do run into her. Who cares if after one day I find myself smiling when she's around? Good situation or not, she's just a girl and one I should start thinking of as my employee.

Laughter from behind catches my attention and I look over my shoulder. A group of girls are coming out of another coffee shop, and it's obvious something is really funny to them. They continue to laugh as they round the corner. Their laughter grows quiet and just before the door to the coffee shop closes completely, I hear the sound of a very familiar voice.

I feel like I'm spying, but I want to make sure I'm not going crazy. It's bad enough I can't stop thinking of her, but now I'm hearing her, too. This isn't good. I take a step toward the coffee shop then freeze when the door flies open and Kelsey steps out holding three coffees in a triangle shape between her hands. She is looking down with a smile and shaking her head.

It's clear she hasn't noticed me. I try to move out of her way, but I'm not fast enough. I swear it is like I watch the whole thing in slow motion: My foot is still in the way, and as I pull it back, Kelsey's leg catches it. She spins around fast, trying to regain balance. It's not going well and as she starts to fall back. I reach out to grab her and pull on her arm too hard; she practically flies at me.

Normally, I would be accepting of situations that bring her body close to mine, but right now all I can think about are the coffees still in her hands, their tops now missing from her gripping them so tight. Like a spring, I jump back. Unfortunately, I don't let go of her arms. All cups of coffee are in the air, headed right toward me.

Shit.

"Hot! Ahhh that was hot!" I shout as I do some stupid hot-coffee dance. I'm leaning forward, tugging on the front of my shirt repeatedly, like that will cool me down. After what feels like hours but is most likely seconds, my shirt is cool enough that I let go of it and look up at Kelsey. Only she isn't there. She's gone.

CHAPTER SIX

Kelsey

Crap.

Double crap.

Sara's going to kill me. If she doesn't do it physically, she'll do it with her eyes. She's the best at speaking with her eyes. *It must run in their family.* She isn't going to have anything nice to say about this, even if all of it was unintentional. She should be playing nice. Not only because Ethan is her cousin, but also because he is going to be my temporary boss. And what have I done? Nothing but terrorize the poor guy.

I push open the door that leads into the bar and poke my head inside, looking left and then right. What if Ethan already called her and told her what I've done to him? Maybe she will think it's funny and we can laugh about it. I take a step inside. *The coast is clear.* She's probably in the office, outlining the necessary points of this meeting. I'll have a few minutes to pull myself together before she comes out.

I love the feeling of being at the bar before we open. Like I have secret no one knows. When it's quiet enough, I can hear the music playing and understand the words. I can actually see the posters of bands who have played here in the past and the neon signs displayed on the walls. Most of the time, I'm so caught up in serving drinks and trying to keep everyone happy, I forget about the small details.

Scratches and chips are visible across the bar top as I run my hand along the surface, heading to stuff my purse in one of the cubbies behind it. It's an "I'm worn and loved" look, the markings of a very popular bar. I hope Sara's parents don't ever try to replace it.

"Day one and he's going to be late!" Sara slams the office door behind her. I jump and cringe at the same time. *Guilty.* She stomps her way to the counter, throws herself onto a stool, and buries her face in her elbow as she leans onto the bar. "You're here before he is. Maybe I should have left you in charge after all."

Her head snaps up.

"Wait," she looks around, then at her watch, the clock behind the bar, and finally on me. "Something's wrong. What happened?"

I show up early and she panics. Shouldn't the boss be happy about that? I shrug then turn the water on. I should get a head start on the side work. Distracting myself is a good idea.

Sara hops off her seat, and I can hear the sound of her black flats slapping against the hard floor as she makes her way behind the bar. She looks nice today. I like her purple top, and the black shorts are cute too. *Wait, those are my black shorts!*

"Why are you here early, Kelsey?" A smile creeps up slowly on her lips and she begins tapping her foot. Her eyes give me a once-over. "And you're wearing a dress … why?"

I focus on mixing the right amount of soap into the water.

"No reason. I was bored sitting at the house so I got ready, went to class, and came here."

"Mmm hmm. So it has nothing to do with my cousin?"

"No, it has—"

"Well, I'll be damned, Kelsey Brian showed up to work before me. Now I've seen it all." Logan struts into the bar like he owns the place and lets out a low whistle. "To what do we owe the pleasure?"

I roll my eyes, but Sara just stands there with a silly smile on her face. Logan has one of those personalities that you can't help but love. Just the tone of his voice and his own smile can improve a girl's mood in less than a second. Not to mention his shaggy, dark blonde hair, blue eyes, and athletic build. He would be a catch in more ways than one. I think Sara is finally figuring it out.

"It's not what, it's who," Sara coos. Warmth creeps up my neck and into my cheeks. Logan's eyes go wide.

"Dude, are you serious? Someone has finally cracked the 'I hate boys' phase we thought would last forever?"

"It's not a phase," I interrupt. "I just find it hard to trust someone now."

Sara's face lights up as she slowly nods her head up and down. "And stop calling us dudes." She laughs, pointing at Logan.

"Wait a minute … does this have anything to do with Ethan?" Logan suggests, folding his arms in front of him.

"Oh, I bet it does," Sarah says.

Logan reaches his arm over the counter, his palm flat, and Sara gives him a high five. *It's like I'm not even here.* How does Logan know about Ethan anyway? I just found out yesterday.

"He called me this morning, wanted to get together but something came up, said he needed a rain check." Logan shares this piece of information as he joins us behind the bar. I continue with my side work and listen to them at the same time.

"Yeah, well, it better be for something good because he said he was going to be late."

He probably went to change his shirt, but I'd be okay with him not changing his shirt and just forgetting about it altogether.

"Hello? Earth to Kelsey!"

I look up from—wait. Was I just staring at the sink water this whole time?

"What's your deal?" Sara asks.

"She knows something," Logan answers.

They both study me with their full attention. I crack under the pressure. It only took two seconds, but it's always hard to keep things from Sara. Then you add Logan, and there's no hope. They make a strong team.

"Alright, so I may have seen Ethan once or twice since yesterday." That sounds good enough. I turn with the intention of filling the sink at the other end of the bar, but Sara grabs my arm. I keep my gaze pinned to the floor.

"And …?"

"And … I might know why he's late?"

"Is that a question?"

My face wrinkles up. I want to avoid this whole conversation. *Treat it just like a Band-Aid, Kelsey. One quick pull and it's over.*

"I may have kicked him in the face, given him black eyes, hit him with my car door, and burned him with coffee right before I got here." I shrug. "Hence no coffee."

Phew. I can breathe now. I pull my gaze off the floor to look at Sara.

Scratch that.

Based on the look on Sara's face, I might not be breathing much longer.

Ethan

"You did what?"

I clear my throat as I walk inside. I don't want to eavesdrop on whatever I interrupted. Kelsey, Logan, and Sara are the only ones here, and all three pairs of eyes focus on me. Kelsey looks like she's about to cry. Sara's eyes practically bug out of her face, and her mouth falls open as she takes a sharp breath. Logan just raises his eyebrows and lets out a whistle, scratches the back of his neck, and walks away. Maybe I should have driven home to get a new shirt instead of buying a new one in town so I could be on time.

"Oh my god!" Sara shouts as she rushes to me. She gushes over me and examines all the viable bruises. It's like having my mom here all over again. When she finishes, her worried eyes meet mine and they quickly turn cold. She whips her head around so fast I swear she snapped something.

"This is all because of you?" she asks Kelsey. Her tone is sharp.

Kelsey is standing behind the bar, frozen. She nods

slowly. Even when she's sad, she's beautiful. I want to hold her and tell her not to worry because it's not her fault. Most of it was just really bad timing on my end. I notice a glimmer in her eyes and my body flinches. I move to take a step toward her, but my cousin cuts me off.

"In there … now!" Sara shouts at Kelsey, pointing in the direction of her office. Wow. So she *can* act like a boss, even though now is not the time, considering this isn't work related. I reach out to stop her.

"Sara, it's not what you think. Wrong place, wrong time is all," I say.

"Yeah, three times?" She huffs. "I don't think so."

I watch as Kelsey follows her with her head hanging low. The front door opens and a guy and two girls walk in, wearing black shirts sporting the BA's initials across the front. One of the women is the redhead from yesterday. Their conversation comes to a stop when they notice me. None of them say anything as they step around me and disappear down the hallway to the left that leads to the bathrooms and break room.

They don't know me. Sara never introduced us yesterday, and the bar is closed. Someone should have questioned why I was standing here. Do they just let anyone walk in before they open?

"So," Logan's voice brings me back to reality and reminds me he's probably the reason they didn't stop me. "You already ran into Kelsey, huh?" He grabs the towel hanging over his shoulder and dries his hands. I let out something that sounds like a laugh, a sarcastic one.

"Yeah, looks that way." I point to my face and move to

stand across from him. He tosses the towel on the counter and then squats down. One by one he begins placing bottles of whiskey on the bar top.

"Kelsey was trying to give us a quick rundown before you came in," Logan says; it sounds muffled since I can't see him.

He stands, putting his palms flat out to either side of him, leans forward, and nods in the direction of Kelsey's office. My head follows his gaze. "I have to tell you, man, I think Sara was faking the whole being mad thing."

"You think?"

"Yep. I've worked with those two long enough to know when they are faking it." He chuckles. "So tell me … did she really kick you in the face? You look like shit."

I pull up a stool and take a seat. I explain my last twenty-four hours to him and he just nods, laughing at the right times. Everything sounds different when I say it out loud. In a way, it looks like I was intentionally trying to be around Kelsey at all those moments.

"Does she know that you told me about your kiss?" Logan asks.

I shake my head. "No. She would kill me."

I've never understood why Kelsey got so mad that day. Yes, I had a girlfriend and it was wrong to be kissing someone else. But I was sixteen. Relationships aren't serious at that age, and this was Kelsey. I had wanted to kiss her since the first day I visited my cousin.

I remember it clearly. I'd been sitting in Sara's parents' living room, setting up my Xbox when Sara came running into the house with Kelsey right behind her, laughing. Sara called me a loser for playing video games, but Kelsey just stood there. We stared at each other for what felt like forever to any sixteen-year-old until Sara dragged her away.

From that moment, the idea of Kelsey has always stirred my body.

CHAPTER SEVEN

Kelsey

"Oh. My. Gosh," Sara squeals the moment she closes the door. She stands in front of me, crossing her arms. A smile appears slowly. "Tell me what happened. It has to be good. Boy, did you do a number on him, Kelsey. He looks like shit." She straightens her arms and grabs each of my shoulders. "Please tell me some of it was an accident from, you know." She wiggles her eyebrows.

Whoa. Freeze. Sara is excited about this?

"I …" I'm so confused. I thought she was bringing me in here to scold me for hurting her cousin. She can't really be serious about Ethan and me fooling around. He's been back for a day.

"Um no. It wasn't like that." I take a step back.

"Then tell me what happened." She can barely contain her excitement. She moves around the desk, sits down, and rests her elbows on the desk with her chin in her hands. "Okay, I'm ready," she says.

I take a seat in front of her and lean back. The chair squeaks. My arms flail in the air as I feel as though I'm about to go down. Sara just watches me until I regain my balance. "You need to buy a new chair," I tell her.

"It's fine. Now tell me!"

As I place my hands on each armrest, I debate whether or not to say anything. I should just sit here with a smile on my face in total silence. I give it a try. Not two seconds go by.

"Uggghhh." Sara groans and throws her head back dramatically. "You're such a pain some days. Just spill already."

Ah, what the heck.

"Alright, so last night Ethan saw me while I was trying to get inside my parents' house and thought I was breaking in. He didn't know it was me. When he tried to pull me off the fence, I kicked him in face, causing his black eyes."

Sara looks confused.

"So he just happened to be in the neighborhood. How did he know where you were?"

I shrug. "I don't know. I guess he lives in the house across from my parents'."

"He bought a house?" she says, shaking her head. "Why would he do that if he's only here for a year? Maybe less."

"I don't know. Maybe he wants to stay longer. Just because he lives there doesn't mean he *bought* the house."

Sara stands and starts pacing around her office. "It just seems weird. He never liked it here and that's a new neighborhood. I can't imagine they would rent houses already."

I don't say anything because she looks deep in thought.

"Anyway." She breathes. "Go on."

"Okay, so then this morning, my car wouldn't start, and I hit him in the face with the door when I got out."

"What was he doing with his face by your door?"

"I have no idea." I laugh. "We never got that far. And then I spilled coffee on him, which again, is why I am coffee-less."

Sara frowns and crosses her arms. "I thought it would be more interesting than that."

I start to apologize for being so boring when Abby, one of the other bartenders, knocks on the door and pokes her head inside.

"Hey, Sara … Kelsey." —she looks away when she sees me— "everyone is here for the meeting."

Sara gestures with her hand for me to get up. When I stand she locks her arm with mine and quietly says, "Try not to hurt him too badly tonight; you're training him."

I glare at her as we walk out of the office to see everyone sitting around the bar. There's only one seat open and it's right next to Ethan. Since Sara will most likely stand to talk during this meeting, I wander toward my seat, and Ethan keeps his head down as I sit next to him.

Sara starts off the meeting discussing pointless stuff: cutting the chit-chat when we're on the clock, people slacking off on their side work, and, of course, showing up to work on time. She jumps right in to the schedule and confirming that she met everyone's requests. People begin passing out this week's copy. The papers come to me. I take one then deliberately pass them to Ethan. Still, it startles us both when his fingers brush mine as he grabs the stack. I jump slightly in my seat, turning to face him. Our eyes meet and neither of us moves. My mouth instantly runs dry, and I have to force the lump in my throat down. Ethan's lips move into a sly grin as he pulls the papers from my hand.

"Hello … hi, yeah, remember me?" Sara says in front of us. *Holy crap.* Wasn't she just standing at the other end of the bar? I pull my gaze from Ethan's and turn until I'm facing Sara. My cheeks are heated as I focus on her and no one else.

"Oh good, you do," she says sarcastically then winks at me. She totally loves this. How embarrassing.

"As I was saying," she continues, "Ethan will be taking over for me." She gives him her best poker face. "Hopefully, he can keep your interest longer than I apparently can." She says it to everyone, but secretly I know she is directing it to me.

It might not be work related, but trust me, Sara. Ethan has plenty of my attention, and I don't see that fading anytime soon.

Ethan

Well, this is one hell of a way to start my new job. Making goo-goo eyes with some chick. *Focus, Ethan.* Kelsey is an employee at the BA. Nothing more. I'm here to succeed at moving some numbers to get my father off my back. Kelsey Brian will be nothing but a distraction. Even as I think it, I doubt myself.

I take my frustration out on the empty keg in front of me, moving it from the cooler to the storage room across the hall, with all the other empty ones. A girl can't be more important than family. It's not possible. But this is Kelsey. She's always been different. As a kid I was never sure why, but now, I'm starting to figure it out.

Sara thought it was best to have her show me the ropes. The night is almost over and I need a break. Being around her is messing with my head and I don't like it. She's almost as unorganized as my cousin, and it drives me nuts that she doesn't write down every order. She claims it's not necessary, but I think it is. Oh, what do I know? I've never had to serve people anything before now. Instead of scribbling down an order, Kelsey just smiles and surprisingly remembers what people want. Everyone in the bar loves her and I know exactly why. She's smart, confident, and as of now, there isn't a dull moment when we are together. It's refreshing, and already I want to spend more time with her. But that's not why I'm here. *Just get the numbers, move some money, and be gone. Don't complicate things by falling for her.*

I finish switching out the keg, then step into the storage room and grab a stack of towels as I head toward the bar. One of the other bartenders, Abby, is blocking my exit. At a quick glance she's cute with a tiny waist and big boobs. But when I look closer, her hair is so light I'm not sure if it's blonde or white and her skin looks like it's about to shrivel up and fall off if she lays in one more tanning bed. She gives me a playful smile as her brown eyes glance over my body.

"So, are you the same cousin who used to visit Sara over the summers?" she asks quietly.

"Yep, that's me."

What does this girl want? I'm not in the mood for this. She takes a step, leaning into me. I can feel her breath on my ear when she whispers, "I'm Abby."

She smells like rotten coconut, and her breath isn't any better. Apparently she's a space case, too. I've been here long enough to know her name. She should clearly know mine now too. Since she's still leaning into me, I whisper back.

"I know, and I'm Ethan, your boss."

She backs off, but her smile doesn't falter. "I know."

"Then get back to work," I say firmly because she isn't figuring this out fast enough.

Her smile falls from her face before she turns to leave. I shake my head as I watch her round the bar, and that's when I see Kelsey watching us. She has a blank expression on her face and it doesn't change after I walk up to her. She looks down to her notepad before she says anything.

"You don't have to be such a dick. You're going to be here for a while and you already have someone who doesn't like you," she says. "It might be a good idea to make a few friends while you're here."

Did she just call me a dick? I'm pretty sure that's violating some kind of rule.

"Employers shouldn't make friends with their employees," I defend myself, resting against the bar, keeping a straight face and looking her in the eyes. Unless Kelsey wants to be friends, and then I'll make an exception. I just won't tell her that.

"Yeah, well, good employees are the ones who enjoy working for someone they like. Someone they can get along with."

She tucks her notepad into her apron and walks away. What? No way is she getting the last word. I come up behind her as she stops and almost run into her.

"We get along. We can set an example. Show everyone what the boundaries are between employer and employee," I suggest. My voice sounds desperate. To spend more time with her or to prove a point, I'm not sure. *Pull it together, man.*

I need to prove a point.

She spins around, her mouth open like she is going to say something, but she stops. She takes a deep breath then looks me in the eye.

"No."

No.

People don't say no to me.

"What do you mean, no?" I growl at her.

Now she's looking at me with pity. She gives me a half smile.

"Look, Ethan, with our history it would be a bad idea. We have never been able to play nice with each other. It happens."

History? We don't have a history. We kissed once and then she freaked out on me. Besides, she's the one who can't play nice. Not me. I'm a nice guy.

"Hey, I'm not the one who kicked myself in the face, hit myself with a car door, and then dumped hot coffee all over myself," I say politely, refreshing her memory.

She scrunches up her face and then pulls her lips into a hard line as she tries not smile. She starts to clear the dirty dishes sitting on the table near us.

"I didn't mean to do any of those things and you know it. I thought we were past that." Her tone is light and playful. I smile as I approach.

"Well," I begin and help her clear the table. "You did get me pretty good. How about if you lock yourself out again, you come get me and we can avoid the cops next time."

For the first time since we started this conversation, I cause her to smile. If she liked what I said, I will absolutely find a way to get her to come to me. We walk the dishes to the bar, setting them on top so the closing bartender can wash them.

"Ok, I will," she says and looks around. "But I don't plan on locking myself out again, so I don't think we will have to worry about that."

I give her my biggest grin. *Yeah ... we'll see about that.*

CHAPTER EIGHT

Kelsey

It was a waste of time showing up to class today. I haven't been able to focus in any of them. It's been two days since I saw Abby flirting with Ethan. I didn't like it and hope I don't have to witness it again. I've never felt that way about any guy. Ever. Not even when Abby walked out of my bathroom that god-awful day I caught Tyler cheating on me.

And Ethan's not your man, Kelsey.

The way she stormed away from Ethan, I knew he shut her down. It took everything I had not to smile at him when he caught me watching. How could I be interested in him again after just a couple days? This just goes to show how unstable my brain is when it comes to choosing someone of the opposite sex.

"Are you even paying attention?" Logan whispers.

I shake my head no.

"Then let's skip out because I'm about to fall asleep."

We quietly grab our bags and sneak out of class without

drawing attention. This isn't good. Ethan has distracted me from the one course I give a rip about. In fact, the other night, I wanted to do nothing but write and Ethan got in the way of that too. This is a bad sign.

"What should we do?" Logan asks. "Maybe go grab a bite or something?"

Food doesn't sound appealing in any way, but I have nothing else going on today and going home to hang out alone doesn't sound fun. And sadly, once again, my mind is more focused on Ethan than plotting some points I could enter to that writing contest.

"Yeah, that's fine."

At my car, I'm a little surprised Logan's making the gesture to open my door. He does this sort of thing for Sara all the time or when we're together, but never for me on my own. Logan really is a sweet guy. Ironically, the moment I think it, he hits me with the driver's door. I stumble backward, my purse slipping off my arm, tossing every item in it across the ground.

"Oh, dude, I'm sorry." Logan kneels down with me as I gather everything up.

"It's alright," I tell him, but he's almost laughing. "It doesn't look like you're too upset about hitting me," I joke back. It's really not a big deal, but then he reaches his hand toward me and I realize why he is laughing. I grab the tampon out of his hand, stuff it deep into my purse, leap into the car, and slam my door closed, praying he doesn't see the blush I have no doubt my cheeks are displaying. This is probably why he's never opened a door for me. Probably had some sixth sense that it would be awkward one way or another.

Hanging out with Logan for a while is fun. He asks about

Sara a bunch, which doesn't surprise me. Those two aren't very good at hiding their feelings. I thought for sure they were going to finally put themselves out of their misery and make things official, but then she up and decided to leave for this trip and didn't even tell Logan. He found out from Ethan. The way he's been talking about her this afternoon only confirms everything I thought: Logan doesn't want her to go.

I pull up to my parents' house around five. I have a plan to accomplish a lot of homework tonight, but after a good fifteen minutes of searching through my purse, backpack, and car for their house key, I give up. I must have lost it when I dropped my purse.

I get out of the car, close the door, and lean against it. I should have made a spare key after the first night. I take a deep breath and glance across the street to Ethan's house, where the front light is on. He did tell me I could come to him if this happened again. I push off my car and head for his house.

I knock once and the door opens. Ethan's in a pair of blue jeans and a simple red t-shirt. His hair looks a little messy, like he's been running his hands through it. At least, I hope it was him.

"Hey, Kelsey, what brings you over?" His voice is shaky, and sounds a tad bit forced or rehearsed, I'm not sure which.

"I, uhh … I lost my key, I think," I say, hoping he'll invite me inside.

"Oh, yeah, come on in," he says, stepping to the side to let me by with a pleased grin on his lips.

The scent of sandalwood and oranges fills the air as I pass him. It's a good smell. One that will forever now remind me of Ethan. Then again, cologne or not, I have a feeling I'm not going to forget about him because right now, my mind has forgotten everything *but* him. If I can't get a locksmith here soon, I might end up doing something completely not in my plans.

My eyes flash from his eyes to his mouth and back. Yep. Kissing is definitely not in my plans, but right now, I might need to add it.

Ethan

No one needs to know that I asked Logan to sneak her house key off her keychain while they were in class. Except he didn't do it while they were in class—instead, he faked opening her door and then knocked her on her ass to get it. He let me know I owed him big time.

"Do you want anything to drink?" I ask her. She shakes her head and sits on my black leather sofa. Okay, so I hadn't thought this far ahead. I was too worried watching her out the window like a creep, hoping she would take me up on my offer from the other night that I almost pulled my hair out. I sit down next to her. She looks at me, tilting her head to the side and gives me a small smile.

"No thanks. I'm just going to Google a locksmith and hopefully I won't be in your way too long."

"Yeah, sure, of course," I say, heading into the kitchen for a glass of water anyway. I can't just stand out there staring at her and doing nothing. If I can't convince her to hang around for a little while, this whole thing will be for nothing. I could just ask her out like a normal guy, but she seems to have her shit together a lot more than me, and I've yet to see signs of a guy in her life being something she's interested in.

"I have a slight problem," Kelsey says behind me in the doorway, leaning with her back against the frame and digging through her purse. "My phone just died and I didn't have time to write the number down. Do you have your phone or an iPad maybe? Anything really."

She shoves her phone back into her purse. I don't understand how anyone can let their phone die in our generation, but right now, I'm not going to question it. I just wish my phone were dead, too, and that I can't remember where my tablet was.

"You can use mine," I suggest, holding my phone out to her.

"Thank you." She takes the phone out of my hand and wanders back into the living room to take a seat on the sofa. Sooner than I had hoped, she's talking with a locksmith. I sit down in the recliner this time as I wait for her to finish.

This would have worked a whole lot better if technology weren't everywhere.

She hangs up and sets the phone on the table in front of her.

"He says it's going to take a couple hours. Is it alright if I wait here?"

Sure is.

"Yeah, that's cool." I look at my watch. It's almost five. "We could order a pepperoni pizza and watch a movie while we wait."

"That sounds great." Kelsey smiles.

I walk into the kitchen to order dinner, and when I come back to the living room, she's settled on the couch, watching TV. I'd expect her to pick some girly show, but instead she chose *Breaking Bad*. She looks good on my couch, in my house. It feels right, and something about that terrifies me. Walking into a room with her in it is nothing like when I join my parents or brothers. Right now, I feel like I can just be me and that's good enough. I don't have to pretend. How did she do that to me after just a couple days?

I take the seat next to her, and from the corner of my eye I can see her body stiffen the moment I sit down. She crosses her left leg and relaxes back into the couch. Her smile is gone and in its place is an expression full of focus.

"This is a good show," I say, filling the silence between us. I don't know what else to say. This is new for me. I never have a problem talking to women, but with Kelsey, everything feels different.

"I think so, too," she says.

Get it together, Ethan.

I act as though I'm adjusting myself to get comfortable and manage to slide closer to her. There's nothing discrete about what I just did, but she doesn't move. I reach my arms above my head to stretch. I'm about to pull a really old-school move—and let's be honest, it rarely ever fails. As I lower my arms to my side I keep my right arm straight and rest it on the back of the couch behind Kelsey's head. At this exact moment it feels like everything in the room falls to silence, except for the bubble of laugher that comes out of her mouth.

I quickly glance at the TV, hoping the show is at a funny scene, but it's not. Kelsey is laughing at me. Talk about blowing a man's ego. I lift my arm off the couch. This isn't working out how I want. Before I can rest my arm back at my side, she quickly scoots under my shoulder and rests her head against my chest. I freeze. Kelsey Brian just made a move on me. I want to jump off this couch and fist-pump my hand in the air. I slowly lower my arm around her to pull her close.

This is exactly how I wanted things to go.

We make it through another episode before the pizza shows up and then quickly devour every slice in the box. I get up to toss the box in the trash, and this time when I sit next to her, I don't hesitate on how far apart we should be.

"Hopefully, the locksmith gets here soon," she says, looking at her phone. I find this funny since earlier she told me it was dead. I want to smile like some lovesick puppy. She wants to be here just as much as I want her here.

"That's okay. You can stay here as long as you need to."

"Is that the same Xbox you had when you were sixteen?" she asks and I follow her gaze to the gray-and-white game box sitting under the TV.

"Yeah, I actually—"

"Can we play something?" She beams, sitting forward on the couch. She wants to play a video game?

"Sure." I get up and turn the box on, giving her a few options. It's been years since I played a game on this thing. I only kept it so I could watch movies with it.

"Let's play this one." She waves a simple car racing game in my face.

I put the disk in the player and hand her a controller. We sit cross-legged on the floor in front of the TV. Occasionally she squeals when she wrecks or turns her car in the opposite direction, but otherwise we're both pretty quiet. We're on the last lap when I make my signature move from all those years ago and cut her off, causing her car to spin out of control. She squeals again and shoves me over.

"You did that on purpose. I was going to win and you knew it." She laughs.

In a moment like this, I have to take advantage of the open opportunity. I give her a slight push back and she grabs my shirt, pulling me toward her as she falls onto her back.

Our faces are inches apart. Our eyes lock and that's when it clicks. She planned this whole Xbox idea. I start to smile, but when she licks her lips, her tongue brushes against my bottom lip. *Shit.*

"This was a bad idea," she whispers right as our lips are about to touch. "We shouldn't get involved with each other." I lean my forehead against hers and let out a struggled breath.

"Why not?" I ask even though I know the answer. I would never force Kelsey into something she didn't want to be a part of, and I know the reasons *I* shouldn't do this, but I don't understand hers. She's never given me any sign she wasn't in to this. Into me.

"We just can't." She places her hand on my chest to push me back. She stands quickly, reaches for her purse then turns for the door. With each step she takes I feel cold. Everything felt right with her in my arms and now she's gone. This is wrong. I kneel, reaching for her before she makes it to the door, but her phone rings and the moment is over.

CHAPTER NINE

Kelsey

What I wouldn't have given for the locksmith to wait just ten more minutes. As I walk across the street to meet him, I glance over my shoulder at Ethan's house. He's leaning against the doorframe, watching me with his arms crossed and a smile on his face. I wanted to kiss him. I want more than just to kiss him. But I can't let myself fall into that again. Into the hope that this time it's real. I can't assume that every guy will turn out like Tyler, but I'm not sure it's a chance I want to take. That, and just the idea of him demands more focus than anything else in my life. I need to be 100 percent focused on writing.

I planned the entire game idea from the moment I sat down on his couch and turned on the TV. Every time I'm around him all the emotions I felt when I was fifteen years old come flooding back. That moment, right before he was about to kiss me, my mind went blank. I know where I'm at in life and what I want, but Ethan makes me forget all that.

I wait patiently as the locksmith lets me into my house, and Ethan watches us the whole time. I know he isn't trying to be creepy. He's only making sure I get inside safely. That's one trait Tyler never had, putting someone else's safety first. I turn to give Ethan a small wave good-bye before I close the door.

I can't let the idea of getting hurt keep me from experiencing something great. Ethan and I—it could be more than great. And eventually I want to have a family and a career as an author. Now is as good a time as any to start balancing the two. I'm going to do it. I'm going to give Ethan a chance.

First thing tomorrow, I'll tell him everything. Lay it all out there and let him make the next move.

* * *

It was hard to sleep last night. My heart raced the entire evening and my stomach fluttered like a child on Christmas Eve. I couldn't wait for morning to get here. Luckily for me, I don't have to wait till the clock hits seven before I get up because the persistent knock at exactly six is hard to ignore. I make my way down the stairs and stand on my toes to look through the transom. A groan slips past my lips as I take a deep breath and open the front door.

"Good morning, Mrs. Mulligan," I greet her and take step to the side. She's holding two coffee cups and a Thermos. "Would you like to come in?"

Mrs. Mulligan stands there for a second but doesn't look at me. Instead, she stretches her neck and looks behind me. Poofy, gray hair fills my vision as she surveys the living room. Finally, her dark brown eyes flash to me and she smiles.

"As long as I'm not interrupting anything," she says with a mischievous grin. I give her my best smile in return.

"Not at all, just a restless night."

She walks past me straight for the kitchen like it's something she does every day. She takes a seat at the round wooden table made for six and starts to fill the cups she brought with her.

"I'd be restless, too, if I were your age and a boy like that lived across the street from me. Do you know much about him?" she asks. I try to not laugh as I join her at the table. She didn't waste any time getting to the point of her visit this morning.

"His name is Ethan Connelly. He's a cousin of my friend Sara."

A startled expression appears on her face and her hand bumps her cup. Some of her coffee sloshes onto the table and she starts to rise. I stop her.

"I'll get you a napkin, Mrs. Mulligan."

"Please, call me Helen."

I grab a towel and return to the table.

"So, is this Max Connelly's son?" she asks.

I nod. I wasn't aware she knew the Connelly family well enough to know Ethan's dad.

"One of them. I think there are three boys total, but I'm not quite sure."

Her mouth twists as she glances out the kitchen window. "And what is he back in town for?"

She doesn't look at me when she asks, but there's something else in that curious tone of hers. Almost as if she thinks she needs to be cautious with the question.

"Sara's going out of town for a while. Ethan's here to help with the bar."

"Ethan?" she asks, her voice loud and shocked. "Of all those boys, he let Ethan come?"

The way she says "let" makes it sound as though choosing him wasn't ideal. I take a sip of the coffee she brought while she fidgets with her mug. Is she having this conversation because she wants to know about her new neighbor or because she's digging for information? I bet my mother filled her in on all kinds of crazy stuff from around town.

"I don't know why they wouldn't pick Ethan."

Helen just nods then waves her hand, dismissing the topic.

We finish our coffee with a much lighter discussions of classes and how living next to my parents has been a delight for her. It sounds like she and my mother are becoming quite good friends.

"Well, I must be going," she says, standing and collecting her Thermos. "See you around, Kelsey. I'm very happy to know you're staying here while your parents are away. Ever since Mr. Mulligan passed, the closeness of friends is important to me."

The idea occurs to me that maybe she and my mother have coffee together often, and that I could fill in for my mom while she is away.

"Of course. Come back tomorrow, same time?"

Her smile grows as she opens the door.

"Kelsey, I'd be hesitant to let that boy anywhere near you. His father was always a snake. I don't like to judge his boys off his behavior, but I don't trust that family ..."

A smile wavers at my lips as I give her a puzzled expression. She doesn't trust Ethan?

"… not after the fit Max Connelly threw at his father's funeral. Men like that only think of themselves and for your sake, I hope he didn't raise his boys that way," she adds.

"I'll make sure Ethan is on his best behavior."

"Good, you can start now. He's on his way over here." She glances back at me. "Maybe you should fix your hair?" She laughs and walks out the door. Sure enough, Ethan is crossing the street with flowers in one hand and a grocery bag in the other. He's giving me the biggest smile he can make.

First Mrs. Mulligan warns me away from him, and now I need to improve my appearance. She's lost her mind. Getting old must suck.

Ethan

After tossing all night, I've finally made a decision. I want Kelsey and I don't care whose rules I break to make it happen. My father can suck it. It's not the most mature attitude to have, but I'm starting to learn that there are more important things in life than gaining my father's approval. Being with Kelsey is worth losing a relationship with him. Then again, I can't lose it seeing as how we never really had one to begin with. My brothers were always his favorites. They did everything he wanted and they did it exactly how he wanted it. I'm starting to think it might be because none of them actually has a heart.

None of that matters now. I'm going to convince Kelsey we should give this a real chance. There's a reason my feelings never went away and I have to find out what made her stop last night. I have to fix it.

There's a spring to my step when I reach the sidewalk

outside the Brians' house. Kelsey is standing in the doorway, wearing a pair of blue, white, and silver pajama pants and a red t-shirt that says The Black Alcove across the chest. Her hair is a mess, in a sexy way, and her eyes light up when I get to the door.

"Good morning, Ethan," she says, taking a step back and waving her hand to gesture me inside. She blushes as she tries to hide the smile on her face.

"Good morning," I say, not caring about the shit-eating grin on my face, too. "These are for you." I hold up a bouquet of colorful flowers and her hand brushes mine when she takes them. When she looks into my eyes, I have to resist the urge to grab her and kiss her. Maybe that would cure the fact my heart both races and slows down each time I see her.

"These are beautiful." She closes the door behind us. "What are you doing up so early?" I follow her to the kitchen where she pulls a vase from a bottom cupboard and fills it with water. I set the bag of groceries I brought with me on the island and take a seat.

"Well, Sara mentioned that you just started housesitting a couple days ago, and I made the assumption that you probably haven't had time to make it to the store." I start unloading the bag. Eggs, bacon, sausage, potatoes, onions, and cheese fill the counter space between us. "I'm going to make you breakfast."

"Can you even cook?" she asks in a flirtatious tone.

"Of course I can cook."

"Okay, but are you any good at it?"

"The best," I say, making my way around the counter to stand in front of her. She freezes and looks into my eyes as I tuck a strand of hair behind her ear. "Why don't you relax, do whatever it is girls do when they get ready for the day, and I'll let you know when breakfast is ready."

A confused expression washes over her face and she looks away. Her lips part like she's going to say something, but then she closes them, nodding before disappearing up the stairs.

I hope she's as accepting of the idea of us as she is to the idea of me cooking breakfast for her. If she is, I just might have to make this a regular morning routine.

CHAPTER TEN

Kelsey

Ethan's here, in my kitchen. Well— my parents' kitchen, but he's here for me. He's making me breakfast and I just—let him. Confessing my feelings should go easier than I thought. I hear drawers open and close from inside the kitchen. I hope he doesn't ask me where anything is; I don't know my way around this house. I should probably start visiting my parents more. Especially with Ethan living so close to them. I glance at the hallway mirror on the way to my room and pause when I see my appearance. A gasp slips past my lips a lot louder than expected.

"Is everything okay up there?" Ethan's voice carries up the stairs. I cover my mouth with my hand and then quickly start smoothing out the frizz. Helen wasn't kidding. My hair looks like a bird's nest.

"Everything's fine," I say when I reach my room. I grab a pair of jeans and a t-shirt on my way to the bathroom.

Quickly, I brush my teeth and my hair, and then apply a light coat of makeup.

Staring at my reflection in the mirror, I take a deep breath. It's not a crime to be into Ethan. He's smart, sexy, and mysterious to me. The fact that he's clearly still into me after all these years is something I can't wrap my mind around.

I haven't been the luckiest girl when it comes to men. I was the other woman for my first kiss, and for my first love, I found not one, but two other woman in our bed. I've been the accomplice and the victim. The next man I date isn't going to betray me. That alone is a huge reason why I need to take it slow with Ethan or stay away from him completely. What's that saying—once a cheater always a cheater? *Please don't let that apply to Ethan.*

Crap. Maybe I shouldn't tell him how I feel.

Closing my door, I casually make my way into the kitchen to find Ethan pulling the orange juice from the fridge. The table is set for two, and there's enough food to feed us for the next week. *Us.* That's so cute.

Crap again.

Make up your mind, Kelsey.

"Hey," Ethan says, catching my gaze. "What do you have planned for today? I thought maybe we could go downtown, take a walk or something. You can show me everything I've missed the last seven years. Maybe we could even head out to the lake for a few hours."

"That sounds great. I can't believe it's been that long. It feels like you've been here the entire time." I take a seat at the table.

"Yeah, crazy, huh?"

Ethan places a glass of orange juice in front of me and

takes the seat next to me. He scoots his chair in and his leg brushes against mine. It sends a tingle that settles in the pit of my stomach. Every time he gets close to me, I swear my body forgets how to act normal.

"So what's new? Are you ready to be finished with college?" Ethan grabs a piece of toast and slathers it with grape jelly before I answer.

"College is good, and yes, I am ready to be done with this degree."

I take a bite of bacon and look down at my plate. I can feel him staring at me so I wipe my mouth just to be on the safe side.

"What's your major?" he asks.

"Accounting."

"Really? I would have figured you'd be a writer one day or make reading a career. I swear, you always had a book in your hands when I saw you."

This makes me laugh. "If you could get paid to be a reader, I'd have totally done that. And yes, I want to be a writer, but I don't think my dad would be very impressed. I still plan to go to school for English, but not right now." I say, shoving more food into my mouth before I share any more information than I need to.

"Your dad … really? I always thought you got along. What did I miss?"

Ethan turns his body to face me, resting one arm across the back of my chair. Something about his soft gaze and immediate interest in my relationship with my father instinctively tells me I can trust him.

"I don't know." I shrug. "One day he was my best friend, the next, he was different. From that day on he chose my brother over me every time. Then when Conner left, I hoped things would get better, but they never did. I thought by choosing accounting and following in his footsteps, the dad I used to know would come back. I miss him, and I can't imagine going the rest of my life not being close to him. Sometimes I wonder if my taking a semester off after graduating high school was the problem, but I don't know."

Ethan nods slowly as if it takes him a while to process my answer. "I actually see why—"

His phone rings in his pocket and he pulls it out, glances at it, and quickly sets it to silence. He grabs another piece of toast and stands. "I … forgot I had some things to do on my house today. Can I take a rain check on that walk?" He heads out of the kitchen, but turns to face me in the doorway. "Accounting major or not, your dad would be a fool not to come around."

Ethan

I should really learn to take my own advice. My father is a fool too, if he won't accept me for who I am. But like Kelsey said, she can't imagine living the rest of her life butting heads with her father and neither can I. There has to be a different way to gain his approval.

I know I made my decision and I chose Kelsey, but I still need to find a balance between her and my father. I can't just straight up tell him I'm done or he'll find another way to pull this off. The real me won't let that happen. My cell buzzes inside my pocket a second time once I'm outside. It's probably a follow up phone call to the text he just sent me.

· · ·

Dad: I'm sending one of your brothers if I don't hear from you in the next twenty-four hours.

Typical. He never asks how my day is or how I'm doing. He just gets right to the point. I'm about to answer the call when I look up to find Tyler Maron leaning against a blue Ford parked across the street in front of my house. He gives me a quick nod in greeting before pushing off the truck with his foot.

"Hey, Tyler, it's been a long time. How've you been?"

"Ethan," he says and pulls me in for a shoulder bump hug and slaps my back. "I heard you were back in town for a while. My dad told me where I could find you. What were you doing at Kelsey's parents' house?"

I figure he knows Kelsey's staying there. Back when we were kids, Sara, Kelsey, Logan, and Tyler were inseparable and they always knew where to find each other.

"Your dad told you where to find me?"

"Yeah, he said, 'That Connelly boy is back in town, causing trouble across from the new Brian home. Haven't seen him in years, not since his father and Sara's couldn't decide who was going to take over that old bar.'"

Tyler chuckles once he finishes his impression of his father and I join in. When the laughter fades Tyler scratches the back of his neck and looks past me.

"Is, uh … Kelsey really watching the house for a few months?"

"That's what she says."

"Is she home now?" He looks nervous and avoids making eye contact with me. Something is up with him and I don't like the idea of him acting like this around Kelsey. If it freaks me out, it will definitely freak her out too.

"Ah … no. Actually, she left early this morning. I was … watering a plant."

Fuck.

I sound like an idiot. Why am I lying to him? It's not like Kelsey and I are together. She should be able to talk to any guy she wants.

"Oh."

Please don't question anything about her car in the driveway.

"Well, that's okay. I'm sure I'll see her later. Are you free tonight? We should meet up for a drink if you are," he says and jumps in his truck, shutting the door before I can reply. I wave from the sidewalk and he drives away. A lot has changed since I've been here and I don't think all of it is positive. Not with Tyler anyway.

A flicker across the street grabs my attention before I head inside. Kelsey's eyes instantly grab mine from behind the curtain she's peeking around. She gives me a slight nod and then disappears. Was she hiding from Tyler?

I don't have enough time to wonder about it before my phone rings once again. I don't even look at the screen before I answer. There is only one person it could be.

My father.

CHAPTER ELEVEN

Kelsey

"On time again?" Sara puts her hand on my forehead. "Nope, she isn't sick," she says to Logan, who's sitting next to her at the bar.

"Hmm." He rubs his chin. "Could a certain new man in town have anything to do with this punctual thing you've got going on?"

He chuckles slightly and Sara giggles. I swat her arm away from my face and walk around the bar to put my purse in the cubby. I can get very little past Sara. When you put her and Logan together, it's like they are one smart-ass person with this creepy power that makes you admit anything and everything with just a look.

"I won't deny it. I'm happy to see Ethan again," I say flatly. But his running off at breakfast a few days ago? Not impressive and not a good sign, considering I haven't seen him since then.

"I knew it!" Sara shouts, kicking her chair back as she

stands and points a finger in my face. "You were into him even when we were kids. Ahhh! This is so exciting."

"Are you just figuring this out?" Logan asks, returning her chair upright.

"No, I always knew. I was just waiting for her to admit it."

"Sure you were." Logan joins me behind the bar. I wipe off the counters as I make my way to the sink at one end and turn on the water. I'll let those two enjoy their moment. If they can ever figure out their own relationship, I could see many double dates in the future. A high squeal comes from their end of the bar, and I look to see that Logan is now tickling Sara from behind.

Why would she want to leave this? Most people are happy when they talk about traveling, but there wasn't a smile on her face when she told me she was leaving. Just a mention that her father said if she wants him to fund it, it's now or never.

"Okay, stop, stop. I need to talk to Kelsey about girl things and you need to finish doing that inventory count in the back." She pushes Logan away and he grins until he's out of sight. God, those two drive me nuts.

"So, you and Logan?" I raise my eyebrows a few times to tease her.

"No, I don't think so. We need to talk about you and Ethan. Do you really think it's a good idea?" She laces her fingers together on top of the bar and gives me a serious look.

"What, him being the manager? I think it will work out fine. Why?"

"No, I'm talking about the idea of you and him. Together. In a relationship. I think it's a bad idea."

"Whoa." I set the rag down, cross my arms, and lean my hip against the counter. "First, we're not in a relationship, and second, five minutes ago I thought you were excited about this."

"That was best friend Sara talking. This is Boss Sara."

"Ohhh, I see. Well, boss, nothing has come up about dating. We're just friends trying to catch up. That's all."

Lies. All lies. I'm totally into him.

"Well, I hope so. He called to tell me he would be working tonight after he made a huge deal last night about not working. I assume it's because of you."

"Really?"

"I trust you, Kels, but the look on your face just now doesn't say 'just friends'."

I want to prove her wrong. Instead, I spend most of the night watching the door, waiting for him to show up. When he finally does, I struggle to keep my eyes off him.

Sara's going to hate me if I screw this up.

Ethan

I should be learning everything I can about this place, but these people seem to think the only thing I know how to do is change a keg or bring them more alcohol. I grab another box of plastic cups from the storage room and head toward the bar. Logan and Kelsey are the only bartenders tonight; Beth and Abby are on the floor. I thought we'd need more people than that, but since it's Monday and the BA closes early, a small staff is all we need.

I'm relieved to have Logan around. There are mostly females employed here, and it's not that I don't enjoy it or that I'm sexist, but it can be overwhelming trying to keep them all happy. The guy I met on my first day was Lucas. He only works every other Saturday, so I don't plan on seeing him much.

I knock on the bar to get Logan's attention. "I moved that keg for you. Do you need anything else?"

If my dad were here, he would be flipping out at my offer. *"Connellys don't do favors for others; people do the favors for the Connellys"* is his favorite saying.

Funny thing is, I'm a Connelly and I like helping other people. I'm not like him.

"No, I'm good," Logan says and tilts his head away from the bar. "What do you think so far? Is this something you can handle?" There's a touch of humor to his voice as he asks me this. He nods toward the corner where Abby is waiting on a group of men. They all look to be about my age and are all watching her every move. She laughs and the entire group does the same.

"I guess that's one way to make tips."

"You'll get to see some pretty unique stuff around here. Especially during the school year. Last fall, some guy came in here every Friday night to sit in Beth's section. He was a student and all so it wasn't anything weird, but he left her at least fifty bucks every week."

"Really, what was he drinking?"

"Water. He finally worked up the courage to ask her out. She said no and the guy hasn't been back since."

I chuckle. "Money can't buy everything."

I lean back against the wall at the end of the bar, cross my ankles, and watch the scene in front of me. Everyone, both customers and employees, seems at ease here. Being in a bar isn't just about drinking. This is where people come to visit, meet up, or cool down after a busy day at work. A lot goes into creating an environment like this. Does my dad know what he would be getting into? If he ever got his hands on that those account numbers, would he take that away from these people?

"You look like you could use a drink," Logan says without looking back at me. He's mixing a rum and coke in front of him and before I know it, he pours it into a plastic cup and hands it to me. "Here, take this to the cooler and relax for a minute."

I reach for it. "The cooler?"

"Yeah, it's sort of our thing here. We can have a drink or two after a certain time, but we usually take it to the cooler to catch a break."

"Why?"

"Why not? Just go."

I stare at him hesitantly for a minute.

"Just do it."

Glancing between him and the drink, I finally give in. It's been a long night and one drink isn't going to hurt anyone.

I push the door to the cooler open and step inside only to freeze when I see Kelsey standing inside with her back to me. She turns when she hears the door, setting down the cup in her hand. Her eyes dart to the matching clear cup in mine.

"Starting this habit early, are you?"

"Looks to be the thing," I say. "What are you drinking?"

"Reds," she says, picking up her cup and finishing it. She steps for the door, but I stop her.

"You don't have to leave just because I'm here."

"I'm not. But it might look weird if someone realizes we're both in the cooler for longer than five minutes."

"It hasn't even been one minute; give me a couple more."

She rubs her arms and nods.

"Sorry I ran out on you the other morning. Something came up, but it was a dick move."

"Yeah, a little bit. Especially since you left me with the dishes." A hint of a smile touches her lips.

I laugh. "I did do that, didn't I?"

"Yeah, didn't you ever hear the rule you cook, you clean?"

"I may have heard of that. I promise next time I'll clean up my mess."

Our eyes lock and her face lights up. Her lips press together as she holds back a smile, but she still nods. "Okay."

I step toward her, because there's no way I'm going to pass on this chance with her. My hand grazes her arms and goose bumps fill the surface, a mixture from my touch and the temperature inside the cooler. I know it's cold in here, but all I can focus on is how Kelsey's body feels against mine and the way her eyes shine as she looks up at me. I have been dreaming about this since the moment I came back. I lean forward and she closes her eyes. The cooler hums mute the sound of my heartbeat. Her hand rests against my cheek, and I can feel the closeness of our lips, almost touching but not quite yet, and that's when my cousin decides she wants to join us.

"I don't know where they are, but I'll bring you a case," she says, holding the door open with her back to us. I grab my cup, placing it inside Kelsey's empty one, and step back from her. She smiles and heads for the door.

"Oh there you are," Sara says, glancing between us. "What are you guys doing in the cooler? Are you crazy? It's cold in here."

As if she were trying to make a point, she shivers. "Ethan,

grab a case of Bud bottles while you in here," she adds quickly before exiting. Kelsey follows right behind her.

With a grin, I grab the brown box. Sara just caught two people in the freezer and acted like it was no big deal we were hanging out in here. Either they all sneak off for drinks a lot or she is a total space case.

Warm air hits me, and Sara is waiting for me on the other side, leaning with her back against the bar and her arms crossed.

"Week one, Ethan," she says, shaking her head. "Seven days and you're already sneaking into the cooler to do what? Play kiss face with my best friend. This is a real business, Ethan. I would think that after attending those business courses and getting a degree you would have figured that out by now. Behavior like that doesn't work for me."

"Hey, I didn't plan for that to happen. She was already in there. I had no idea."

"And what? You thought you two would just warm each other up?"

"Sara, it wasn't like that," I say with a defensive tone.

She releases a long sigh before hanging her head in front of her.

"Look, I kind of had a feeling things with you and Kelsey would, well … I don't know. I just had a feeling, and it turns out I was right." She looks down and fidgets with her hands. "Kelsey is my best friend and you're my cousin. Promise me you will get to know Kelsey better before you jump into anything. I don't want either of you getting hurt."

Get to know Kelsey better. I will do everything I can to make that happen. And I am not going to waste any time doing it. I want her. I want every part of her.

There's just one problem. I still haven't figured out how I am going to make a relationship with her and get my father off my back.

"Absolutely," I say when she gives me hug. Sara heads in Logan's direction, passing Kelsey as she does so. My view lingers a bit as I watch Kelsey rinse some glasses in the sink.

If I do what my father wants and Kelsey finds out, I'll never stand a chance with her. If I continue this with Kelsey, I'll never get the kind of relationship with my father that I want. One has to mean more to me than the other, and it scares me that losing an opportunity with Kelsey weighs on me just as much as strengthening what I have with my father.

CHAPTER TWELVE

Ethan

Come on, come on. Stop talking already.

I watch in complete creeper fashion until the moment Mrs. Mulligan closes her front door. Then, I quickly head for Kelsey's. If mornings together are all we have right now, then I am going to make damn sure I am at her house to make breakfast for her every day. I laid awake thinking about my situation a lot last night and came to a conclusion. I won't let anything happen to Sara's bar, and my father isn't going to hear a word of it because I'm not going to let him find out. I'm going to lie to him. Sara will keep the bar, I'll end up with Kelsey, and my father will be off my back. It's the perfect plan.

Kelsey spots me from the doorstep. That's one smile I could get used to seeing every day. I take the porch steps two at a time.

"Hey you."

"Hey yourself." She quickly looks away as redness fills

her cheeks. She tucks a strand of hair behind her ear and then gestures for me to come inside. Damn, she's beautiful.

"I was thinking, if you have time today, I could cash in that rain check and we could hang out."

Hang out, really? Was that my best line?

"Look Ethan, last night in the cooler was … well, I don't know exactly. But you didn't even try to talk to me the rest of the night—I actually think you were avoiding me, and I'm not the kind of girl who likes to play games. Either you like someone or you don't. If you like them, you act like a normal human being around them. If you don't like them, don't lead them on."

She crosses her arms, which pushes up her chest. The other day she had a wicked cute "I just woke up" look. Today, she's completely ready in a pair of blue jean shorts, a pink tank top, and a plaid shirt. Her hair is curled and pulled to side, and her soft golden eyes are the best part about her. When I look into them, that's when I realize I've been caught staring. I do nothing to hide my pleased reaction.

Her hip pops to the side and she rests her hand on it.

"Really, Ethan? I give you the 'no games' speech and you choose that exact moment to check me out." Kelsey rolls her eyes and starts to open the door. I grab her wrist and turn her to face me.

"No games. Not this time. I'm sorry. Give me one more chance and I won't screw it up. Not this time. I promise."

Taking in a deep breath, Kelsey's gaze roams down and then back up my body. I'd be lying if I said those eyes didn't make every inch of me crave her. When she pulls her bottom lip into her mouth and bites on it, it takes every ounce of self-control not to kiss her.

"We'll take it slow." She says and nods.

An ear-to-ear grin takes over my mouth, and I spin for the kitchen. My cooking always wins everyone over.

"But I have class today, in twenty minutes, so breakfast will have to wait for another day."

I stop dead in my tracks and pull myself together before I turn around to let her see the disappointment on my face. *Who takes classes at eight in the morning?*

"Can I drive you?"

"I can drive myself, but thank you for offering." She heads for the stairs.

I can't let her get away this easily. There has to be something I can do to spend more time with her. Today. Not later. I don't want to wait. If I'm actually going against all the rules my father set, either I'm all in, or I need to back out now.

"I think … I'll drive you."

Kelsey pauses and looks over her shoulder.

"And then I'll pick you up for lunch. Maybe even give you a ride to work. We can tell everyone we decided to carpool."

Her lips twitch as she holds back a smile. Finally, she hangs her head in defeat.

"Give me five minutes."

I get out of my truck for the third time. This girl has me so worked up I can't even make the simple decision to sit or stand while I wait for her to get out of class.

The doors to the Littman Building open and students pile out. I spot Logan first; his six-foot build towers over most everyone. When the crowd clears, my eyes fall on Kelsey. She's so incredibly petite next to Logan. She's got her arms crossed over the books in front of her while her hair blows in the wind. Logan nudges her with his shoulder, and she tosses her head back as she laughs. I straighten my stance as jealousy floods me. I want to be the guy who makes her respond that way. Kelsey bumps his shoulder back, and I force myself not to look away. Jealousy is new for me and I don't like it.

"Kelsey, Logan, hey," I say when they are close enough. Her eyes are focused on me now.

"Ethan, we were just talking about you," Logan says and nudges Kelsey *again*.

"We were not." She widens her eyes at Logan and mouths something to him, but I can't see what.

Great, they even have inside jokes.

"Nothing bad anyway." Kelsey looks back to me and blushes. She does it every time our eyes meet, and every time it makes me want her more.

"I'm going to head out, but I'll catch you both tonight at work, right?" Logan gives me a fist bump and then quickly gives Kelsey a side hug before heading in the opposite direction. I know he lives close to campus and walks to class every day, but I still feel a tad bit like a dick for not offering him a ride. Kelsey clears her throat and then those brown eyes meet mine once more.

Like I say—I only feel a tad bit bad.

Kelsey

"So where are we going?" I climb inside Ethan's truck and he sets my books on my lap after I buckle my seatbelt.

"It's a secret." His face lights up and he closes my door. I watch as he jogs around to the driver side. My stomach flutters immediately when he flashes me a smile from the front of the truck.

"You're still a fan of surprises, right?" He starts the truck. "Because if you're not, then I'm screwed."

I let out an embarrassing laugh slash snort at the worried expression on his face. I slap a hand over my mouth and nod with wide eyes. If I keep making noises like that, he might change his mind.

"Good."

He backs his truck out of its parking spot and pulls off campus. He takes a right, then a left. We pass The Black Alcove and right when I'm about to kill the awkward silence, he slows to a stop in front of Sara's and my apartment building. When he kills the engine, I know my face reads nothing but confusion.

"We're here." Ethan beams at me. "Wait, I'll get your door." He jumps out and again, I watch him jog around the truck to my door. *What is he up to?*

My door swings open and he tosses my books from my lap to the now-empty driver's seat.

"No studying on this date." He looks serious. I nod like I have no choice but to do what he says. Ethan slips his hand in mine and gently pulls me from the truck.

"Wait here."

This excited behavior completely baffles me, so I try to sneak a peek at what he's pulling from the back of his truck. The tailgate slams shut and he looks over the bed with a grin that practically makes me forget how to breathe.

"You planned a picnic for lunch?"

He laces his fingers with mine as we cross the street. I've lived in this apartment for two years now. Not once can I remember having lunch in the park. This memory with Ethan will be one I never forget.

"I planned a picnic in the park for our *first date*."

We stop under a tree that provides shade but also has enough sun peeking through the branches to keep us warm. Ethan spreads out the blanket and takes a seat. One by one he takes out sandwiches, bottled water, baked barbeque chips, and a bag of cookies. Next he pulls out some plates.

"Are you going to sit down or just watch me?"

A picnic might sound like a cheesy move, but when you're in the moment and a gorgeous guy is offering you a turkey sandwich with a huge smile on his face that you know you put there, it's the sweetest moment in world, and I wouldn't change a thing.

CHAPTER THIRTEEN

Ethan

The next morning comes fast, and as I listen to my phone vibrating against the nightstand, I know I can't avoid my father any longer. It's been a week and a half since my successful picnic in the park. Every morning I go to Kelsey's house and make breakfast, I pick her up for lunch, and then we spend almost every night working together. The only way things could get better is if we had a night alone … and if my father would stop calling. I've responded via text with things he wants to hear, but I have to answer his calls eventually. I'm avoiding him while I figure out what to say. Texting is much easier.

"I haven't found the numbers you need," I answer in a tone that sounds similar to his everyday one. Cut right to the chase. I don't care what he has to say anyway. I'll say whatever it takes to keep my brothers away from Wind Valley.

"So, you do know how to answer a phone," he says. He doesn't sound concerned, only annoyed. "Your brother is packing a bag and leaving today. You can expect him tonight. When he arrives, you can come home. I have different plans for you, ones that don't require so much responsibility."

Fuck.

"That won't be necessary. I've got everything under control here. My lack of response to your phone calls has been due to nothing but hard work to find what you want."

Complete silence except for my father's heavy breathing fills the phone line. I imagine he's standing in his study in a black suit. He has one hand in his pocket while the other holds a finger just above the end call button of the phone sitting on the corner of his desk. He'll take his hand from his pocket and drill his fingers against his desk, glancing up to the fireplace and back to his fingers three times before he makes up his mind. I've seen him do this more times than I can count. It's the moment he's debating whether he's hearing the truth.

"If you haven't found what I need, then you haven't been working hard enough. You do realize, son, that I can send one of your brothers there to watch over you without taking your spot. Someone to keep you in line while you are there. We don't know exactly how long Sara will be away, so you need to act fast, and mistakes are something I can't have you making."

"Yes, sir, I understand you could do that. But my sudden appearance after all these years has already raised some suspicion. I think it's best to hold off on sending anyone else. Drawing attention isn't what you need right now."

At this point everything I've said is100 percent bullshit. I know Sara wants to ask more, but she doesn't. She has always been a big believer in family and sees nothing but the best in me. If only I could see what she does, maybe I could stop my father. I'm in too deep now. No matter what happens, I'll end up looking like the bad guy.

"Just keep going the way you have been, and I'll make the best decision. Keep your eyes open. You never know how easily things can change."

Like always, he doesn't say good-bye once he's spoken the last word. An eerie feeling flashes through me. More than likely, he's still sending one of my brothers. I sure as hell hope he sends Lance, because if he sends Ben, there is no telling what could happen.

Growing up, Lance always found a way to look out for me. As long as he was at the top of our father's list, Ben couldn't have cared less if I was in trouble or not.

With two fingers I pinch at the nerve between my eyes. What am I going to do? I had this all figured out days ago. Now, my father's words keep playing in my head.

Keep your eyes open. You never know how easily things can change.

I could just let one of them take over. It would be easier, but helping my father doesn't feel right. I can put it off, my brother won't. I have to figure something out. Whatever my father has planned isn't good. And there is only one way I know to protect Kelsey. I have to cut all ties with her beyond an employee/employer relationship until I know what's he's going to do.

Kelsey

The next few days pass in a blur. After about a week, I finally worked up the courage to cook for Ethan. I woke up one morning to make Ethan a breakfast casserole, but he never showed. The morning after that, another no show. I called him, but he didn't answer. One morning I went as far as to go over to his house to make sure everything was okay. I know he pretended he didn't hear me knocking on the door. I'm not crazy. Something's going on and I want to know what it is. It's incredibly odd to me to just stop talking to someone with no explanation. I want one.

I deserve one.

Tonight is Sara's going-away party, and being held at the BA, it's the perfect place to run into Ethan and ask him what his deal is.

I'm back in our apartment getting ready with her. She leaves tomorrow and it plain out sucks. For me. Not her. I slide my feet into the black pumps that I save for special occasions. They don't happen very often so tonight will make it the second time I have ever worn them. *I hope I can remember how to walk in them after I've been drinking.*

"Kelsey, hurry up, let's go!" Sara hollers at me from down the hall. I check myself one last time in the full-length mirror behind my door. My little black dress hugs my body amazingly, my hair is curled to the middle of my back, and my shoes make my legs look long and lean. Hopefully, this outfit can get Ethan to confess what's been going on with him. I smile at myself and grab my red clutch off the dresser. This dress better do more than get him to confess—it better grab his attention and hold it there all night long.

I've spent more time than any girl should obsessing over a boy. After considering forgetting everything that involves Ethan, I came to the conclusion that I'll just go with whatever he has in mind. I'm not going to initiate anything, but I won't say no if he brings it up. I like the way I feel when I'm around him. He opens doors, he makes me laugh, he's got a bit of a romantic side to him, and he always smells good. He's got a great smile and a great body, which is a huge plus. All the bad just disappears when I'm with him. Any stress I have is gone and nothing could make me happier. Unless, of course, he stops avoiding me. That would totally make me happier.

"Oh. You look amazing!" Sara squeals. She's waiting impatiently by the door, wearing a red, ruffled dress that falls to her knees, with nude heels. Her blonde hair is straightened down her back, and she has a black clutch in her hands.

"You look amazing as well," I tell her as we lock the door and walk outside. The BA is directly across from our apartment building. Beth, one of the other bartenders, lives in the apartment below us. We usually cut through the park when we walk to work, but not today. Heels and grass just don't mix very well.

The entire place is full of people when we arrive. Most are here for Sara while others are regulars. Either way, her eyes begin to fill with tears at all the people who have come to see her off.

"It's about time you showed up," Logan hollers as he leaps up the steps to guide Sara to the bar. She waves over her shoulder at me as they walk away.

I recognize almost everyone here tonight, but one person stands out. I focus on each step I take to be sure I don't fall in front of him. He approaches me too, staying calm and collected with a smile on his face. I wish I had that much confidence when it comes to me.

"Hey, Kelsey." He leans in to speak into my ear over the music. "You look beautiful tonight."

I blush.

"Thank you." I'm obvious about letting my eyes take in the sight of him. Ethan has on a pair of dark blue jeans that fit him loosely, with a brown belt and a black button-down shirt he has tucked in. He looks handsome and I can't hide the smile on my face.

"Do you want to get a drink?" he asks.

"Yes."

He places his hand at the small of my back, leading me to the bar. My nerves are all over the place, and I already know I'm going to need more than one drink to make it through this night.

"You look stunning tonight."

"Oh really, I'm shocked you noticed what with all the avoiding you've been doing lately."

Ethan gazes at me from the corner of his eye before waving at Lucas. "Can I get a Bud

and Kelsey will have a …" His left brow raises waiting for my response.

"Reds, please," I say because I haven't lost all my manners. Although he doesn't really deserve any right now. I planned to come here and grab his attention. I never said I was going to be nice about it.

Lucas chuckles as he hands us our beers.

"Thanks," I say, quickly stepping away, fully prepared to leave Ethan wanting more.

"I'm sorry, Kelsey."

I stop. "You seem to be saying that a lot these days, Ethan, and you haven't even been here that long."

"I know, I just … I have a lot going on and I'm not sure how I want to deal with it." He takes a drink from his beer, pinning his eyes on me. "I know what I *want*, but wants and needs are two very different things."

My heart thumps louder. He's never actually done anything to hurt me. But the way he's acting isn't a good sign. It's not something I want to mess with. The way he said *wants and needs* makes me think he's hiding something. And although I know I should stay away from him, a huge part of me wants to know what it is he won't tell me, and deep down, I know that's the part of me that's going to win. It's the part of me that's willing to chance getting hurt again for Ethan.

Ethan

From the moment she steps through the door, Kelsey has my full attention. Her black dress is tight on her body, showing off every last curve, and I love it. She looks beautiful and hot as hell, and there is no way I'm going to let any other guy in the place get near her.

I've been back and forth for what feels like a zillion times. Screw it all to hell and be with Kelsey, or stay away convincing myself it's for the best? Right now, Kelsey is definitely weighting my decision toward option one. I can't even look her in the eyes without my mind screaming, "Fuck it, just be with her." Then I think about how far into helping my father I am and I freeze up. I have no idea what I should do.

"Dude, Sara looks smoking hot tonight, don't you think?" Logan asks me. We're leaning against the bar, resting back on our elbows as we watch the crowd. More specifically, the girls as they dance together, capturing everyone's attention. My face wrinkles up and I feel like I'm going to be sick.

"Yeah, no ... that's my cousin. Nothing hot going on

there, my friend." I push myself off the bar, set my beer down, and then head for the dance floor. I watch Kelsey as she moves her hips to the song and laughs with my cousin.

I pause, debating my actions one more time, but one glance in my direction and everything that isn't Kelsey disappears. She jumps when I come up behind her. My hands shake as they rest on her hips, and she turns around slowly, wrapping her arms around my neck. She continues to move her hips from side to side until we have a rhythm together. I can't imagine a moment when I've ever been happier than I am when I'm around her.

"It's hard to do the right thing when what I want most is what I need most," I say into her ear.

Her body stiffens. "It's hot in here, right?" She fans herself with her hand, pulling away but leaving her hand in mine.

"Let's go cool off," I suggest, lacing our fingers and tugging her toward the bar where the crowd is thin. I lift my hand in the air to get Lucas's attention and ask for two waters. He sets them in front of us and Kelsey immediately starts to chug hers. There's a glow off her skin from hours of dancing, and her hair is now pulled up. She turns, leaning her left arm against the bar, and smiles up at me. I reach up to place a stray hair behind her ear.

"I have two things to say to you, Ethan Connelly." She is slurring her words only slightly.

I chuckle.

"And those are?"

"I just want you to kiss me already."

I grin and lean closer. "The other?"

"I'm really glad Sara chose you to run her bar while she's gone."

And just like that, reality returns. When Kelsey finds out the real reason I'm here, she'll hate me.

"Oh, you two are sooo cute." Sara comes up quickly on Kelsey's other side, almost running into the counter, then leans away from the bar, holding on with one hand to look around Kelsey to me. Logan comes up behind her to steady her. "It's such a good thing your dad picked you to come help me and not one of your brothers," Sara says, winking at Kelsey and looking back to me. "Before you know it, you're going to be marking the schedule so all your shifts can be together. You better be a good boss to her, or Logan will beat you up." She slurs a few of her words worse than Kelsey did, but I hear them.

Like clockwork, my phone buzzes in my pocket. Pulling it out, I glance down to see my father's name. I excuse myself to use the restroom, but I don't go there. Instead I leave. Until I figure out what I'm going to do and can stick with it, the farther away I am from Kelsey, the better. For both of us.

CHAPTER FOURTEEN

Kelsey

Sara's been gone for a couple weeks and I've hated not having someone to talk to. Especially with the whole Ethan fiasco. I pretended like things were fine when she left because I don't want her to worry.

The first part of her trip will be in the United States so she promised to make at least one visit back home before she flies to Paris. *Lucky.* Here I am, lying on my parents' couch with a fresh batch of chocolate chip cookies, watching reruns of *Friends*, avoiding the homework I have for class, and dreading the shift I have to work tonight.

After Ethan's disappearance at Sara's going-away party, I've officially decided to cut off of any chance he may have with me. Who cares if he's too good looking for his own good and has a great smile? I don't play games and Ethan has shown pretty damn well that he is great at them.

For the most part, we have kept our distance at work. I'm pretty sure he scheduled it that way, which has resulted in fewer shifts for me. He irritates me to no end these days. Some days he is nice to me and other days he is a complete jerk. I thought he liked me, but I was extremely mistaken. He made that clear when he stopped showing up for breakfast and when he left me at Sara's party. Not that I was thinking clearly that night anyway. *Come on, Kelsey. He isn't a trustworthy person. Once a cheater, always a cheater, right?* That's probably why he disappeared. *Damn it.* Why am I still thinking about him?

At least at work, it's not just me. Things are off to a rocky start with everyone else at the bar too, and have only grown worse. Ethan is taking this temporary takeover way out of control. He told Beth to save her personal problems for off the clock when she was explaining to me why she needed to trade a shift. Logan showed up two minutes late one day and Ethan was ready to fire him on the spot. Logan, his one and only friend. The guy who, after everything, still invites Ethan to shoot hoops twice a week.

His behavior isn't the only crap thing we've got going on —it's his rules on our dress code, too. We're no longer allowed to wear jeans or casual clothing to work—black dress pants and black shoes only and girls must wear their hair pulled back. I accepted that last one, but the rest is just crazy and the list just keeps growing. I understand looking professional, but this is a bar. It's supposed to have a laidback feel to it.

His rules and attitude have been so bad, the others have been coming to me, asking me to do something about it. What can I do? Sara didn't leave me in charge. She picked Ethan and now we're all suffering. I kind of miss the nerdy boy who was sweet to me. He was kind, funny, and cared for others way more than he should have. Now, I can sum him up in one word. *Jackass.*

The sound of my phone vibrating on the glass coffee table startles me. I point the remote to the TV to put it on mute and grab my phone with the other hand. Logan's name flashes across the screen.

"Hey, Logan, what's up?"

"Okay, so I had this idea," he says.

"Why are you whispering?" I ask. He ignores me and goes on.

"Tonight when it gets dark out, like dark enough you can't see anyone, you sneak out of your parents' house and slash his tires then hammer a note to his front door that tells him to 'get out of town or else.'"

Oh geez.

I can't help but laugh. We would never be that fortunate.

"Even if I thought this idea was a good one—which I don't, by the way, but I have to say you're ideas are getting more creative—what happens when he wakes up to my hammering on his door?"

"You run, Kelsey. Duh."

"Right. You do remember what happened the last time he caught me sneaking around someone's house? It didn't end well for him," I point out.

"Exactly!" Logan shouts into the phone.

"He isn't that bad. We don't need to threaten his life. Besides, aren't you still friends with him?" I ask.

"Outside work, yeah. But at work … come on, you've seen him at work. It's like working for that Bain guy in *Batman*, Kelsey. We're all scared to screw up. I know you are too."

"Stop acting like such a wimp, Logan." I push myself off the couch and catch the sight of myself in the mirror at the bottom of the stairs. *Whoa hair, calm down.* "So, what is the real reason you called?" I ask as I try to fix my fuzzy hair while holding the phone with my shoulder.

"Oh. Uh … that was my real reason for calling."

"Yeah, okay." I catch myself rolling my eyes in my refection. "You call me every day that you don't see me in class. Sara told you to check up on me, didn't she? Typical."

Logan's laughter only confirms it.

"Good-bye, Logan."

"Bye, Kelsey, see you at work tonight."

Poor Logan. He has it bad for Sara and is so worked up over her absence. I turn for the stairs and pause mid-step when I hear a loud banging noise from outside. I open the front door and poke my head out. Ethan is inside his garage, standing over a motorcycle, shaking his head. His hands are on his hips and he spins to kick the tire and then yells at the bike. He must sense someone is watching him because he snaps his head right in my direction. I close the door quickly, but there's no doubt he saw me.

As much as I don't want to do anything nice for him, an idea comes to mind. Maybe if I can find someone to fix his bike, he'll be in a good mood for my shift tonight. I send a quick text to Logan, telling him what I saw, and then run up the stairs to work on my paper for that column contest before I have to get ready for work.

Someone's going to knock some sense into Ethan. If it's not Logan, it's going to be me. And there is no time like tonight to start.

. . .

Ethan

This stupid piece of shit bike still won't start. I've been working on it for hours, trying to let off some steam. My dad is being a dick. *You're not trying hard enough, Ethan. Do better, Ethan. Don't make me replace you with your brother, Ethan.* Just hearing my father say my name makes me want to hit someone or something. I am so sick and tired of not being good enough in his eyes.

Sara hasn't been gone that long. What does he expect me to find? It's not like I could be snooping around while Sara was still in town. It was bad enough when Kelsey opened her mouth about my living arrangements. I know Sara thinks I'm buying the house. My cousin drilled me with questions until I gave in and told her I am thinking about staying here permanently.

I don't even care about hurting anyone's feelings anymore. I just want Max Connelly to tell me I did something right or maybe even that he's proud of me. Or I could just tell him to fuck off and be done with it. I'm starting to like that idea more and more.

I was really hoping to get this bike to start so I could go for a long ride where no one can bother me. Take some time for myself. But that's not going to happen. This piece of junk refuses to start.

A reflection off the front of the bike catches my eye and I follow it. Kelsey is standing in her doorway, watching me. She jumps back and closes the door, but my eyes remain glued to that spot for a while. She doesn't appear again.

I rub my fingers over my eyes. My neighbor is another problem for me. Things would be so much easier if I dropped everything my dad wants and did what I want, which is to get to know her better. But I can't, not without hurting her. Maybe I don't know what I want and that's why I haven't done anything. No, that's a lie. I know exactly what I want. I just don't know how to get it without letting someone down.

I step out of the garage toward Kelsey's house, but a black Ford on lifts pulls up in front of my driveway. Logan waves at me through the window and jumps out.

"Hey, man," he says, walking over to me with his hands in front pockets and taking a look around. "I heard you were having a little bike trouble. Mind if I take a look?"

"Kelsey called you, didn't she?"

He nods. "Yeah."

I step back toward my bike. "It won't start. I've been out here most of the day and I can't figure out why," I tell him.

Logan walks around the bike slowly and stops in front of the toolbox. "Is this cool?" he asks, pointing at it.

"Be my guest. I'll go grab us some waters," I say before heading inside. I'll have to remember to thank Kelsey. She didn't have to send anyone to help me, but I'm glad she did. I open the fridge and pull out a couple bottles. The sound of a motorcycle roaring to life comes from the garage.

"No way," I say, stepping outside and handing Logan a bottle.

"It was an easy fix," he says as I grab my helmet, ready to take it for a spin. "So what's the deal with you and Kels? I'm going to be honest. You've been a dick to everyone since the day Sara left, and somehow Kelsey feels enough kindness to help you out."

I shrug and look away from him. "I can't tell you. But I'll be sure to thank her later, and thanks for fixing my bike."

CHAPTER FIFTEEN

Ethan

I hate the way everyone is walking around the bar, pretending like I have a disease. They're all going out of their way to stay away from me. At first I thought it was weird that I hadn't spoken to anyone since I got here, but it isn't until I come out of the office and watch Beth and Abby scatter like the building is on fire that I figure it out. All in different directions, too, and any direction that doesn't include toward me.

I head straight for the end of the bar where Abby is working. The moment I get to the end, she turns around and walks to the other, all without even a glance in my direction. I study each girl and can't find a single clue to what's going on.

"Hey, Ethan, is something wrong?" Logan gestures toward Beth with a bar glass. "Or did she do something wrong?"

"No, I just can't figure out why my employees are avoiding me. I haven't done anything new lately that would piss them off." I pull up a seat in front of him.

"Yeah, women are like that. I'll probably go half my life

not knowing why Sara or Kelsey is mad 70 percent of the time they are around me. It's just how they work—one minute they're calm and couldn't care less. The next minute …"

He clears his throat.

"The next minute, you never know what they're going to do." He chuckles then walks away.

I spin on the seat to see what caught his attention. My eyes about pop out of their sockets when I find Kelsey standing in the doorway, a beaming, white smile on her face. Her hair is pinned up into a messy bun. The Black Alcove t-shirt she's wearing is tighter than normal, showing off her every curve and she is wearing a … mother fucker, she is wearing a skirt. One that is way too short for the public eye. If it's getting to me this fast, it's getting to every other man in this bar too. I take a breath and attempt to control the groan in my throat. This woman knows how to test my patience.

In two quick strides I'm at her side. "What are you wearing?" I ask in the calmest tone I can handle. My hands are clenching at my sides, and when I hear a whistle, I know it's directed toward her. My breathing picks up as I wait for her reply and control my urge to punch the mystery fucker in the face.

Kelsey shrugs and glances down at her chest.

"Um, it's our required uniform, Ethan."

"That is not required." I point to her outfit. "You should be wearing black pants and, let me guess, you shrank your shirt in the dryer?"

"No, I bought a size smaller and I didn't feel like wearing pants today."

"You didn't feel like wearing pants?"

"That's what I said." She smiles again.

"Well," I growl at her and point to her skirt, "that sure as fuck isn't going to work for me."

"Well ..." She rolls her eyes and looks away. "You're going to have to make it work. I'm not changing."

I stand there completely dumbfounded as she walks away. Heads turn as she greets a few people on her way to the jukebox. I watch her hips sway back and forth to the music. *That skirt is way too short*. It reveals her delicious long legs, and when she leans over the jukebox to press a few buttons, my mind starts to wander to places it really shouldn't go right now. I can do this. I can let a couple of rules slide for one night.

She turns back around and gives me a wicked, happy smile. Somehow she managed to learn that when it comes to me, she can get away with anything. I'm just happy she followed one rule and kept her hair pulled back. At least she listened to something I said.

The music switches to a new song and "Sour Cherry" by The Kills plays throughout the bar. I smile back at her, approving her choice of music. From the hoots and hollers it sounds like I'm not the only one who enjoys this song. Right at that moment she reaches up and pulls her ponytail out of her hair and shakes her curls loose down her back.

Fuck. This is not happening.

Kelsey

Before I focus too intently on the fumes blowing out of Ethan ears, I quickly start to chat with some regulars and collect their drink orders. I pick up a few empty bottles as I weave between tables on my way back to the bar. I can feel his eyes burning into my skin. *I can do this. I can do this.* He's budging on the rules, so this is a start.

"Girl, I can't believe you are testing him right now. Logan said he had a hot temper earlier today, and the rest of us have been doing everything we can to stay clear of him. Then, here you walk in, acting like you own the place." Beth laughs and shakes her head. We both glance toward Ethan, who's now standing with his hands on his hips and his head hanging to his chest. *God, he looks so cute when he dresses up. For once I'd like to see him just relax here. He might be a lot happier if he didn't take everything so seriously. I can't imagine Sara giving him any lectures before she left. Maybe he needs someone to help him in a non-work-related way.*

I could do that.

What would he do if I marched right up to him and kissed him? He sure as shit isn't going to make a move. Damn it, Kelsey. Stop that.

"I sure hope whatever you have planned works out for both your—oh shit, here he comes." Beth is gone before I can fully process what she just said. *How did I miss him strutting over here when I was staring at him? Oh right. I was imagining kissing him.*

"Kelsey, might I have a word with you?" Each slow word sounds practiced and forced.

Crap. I hadn't prepared for this reaction. *I mean, I knew this was going to happen, but I never planned how I would react.*

"I—"

"Ethan, I need some help behind the bar. Would you mind talking to Kelsey later?" *Relief instantly takes over at Logan stepping in just in time.*

"You need help with three customers?" Ethan asks.

I glance at Logan, who looks back at the customers then grins at Ethan. "Just go easy on her, please." He chuckles and returns to his spot behind the bar.

Well, that was a poor job of saving me. I'll have to warn Sara about this. Logan is a horrible defender of best friends. He was the one who wanted to devise a plan against Ethan. Clearly, I'm the only one who will actually mastermind it. As slowly as I can muster, I turn to face Ethan. When I meet his heated stare, I bite my lip and hold back a smile. *At least it's kind of working.* I shrug.

"We can talk in my office." He turns for the door with me right behind him.

When the door clicks closed and I hear the twist of the bolt, I step deeper into the office and cringe as I lean against the wall. *I got this.* I'm not scared of Ethan.

But I am surprised when he turns around and a sneaky grin appears on his lips. He stalks over to me and stops once we are toe to toe. Damn, he's close. I can smell his musky and woodsy scent that I can't get enough of. He's so close I can see how soft his skin is from his shave this morning. The mint on his breath focuses me fully on his lips. *Oh god.* Have I always been this attracted to him?

"I can't let you go back out there, Kelsey. Not dressed the way you are."

"Why not?" I cross my arms and look away from him. "I'm wearing the same outfit we used to *always* wear, Ethan. And no one had a problem with it before. Casual is friendly and approachable. You're just going to have to let some things go." I reach to move him out of my way, but instead he grabs my wrist and stops me. I freeze and take a deep breath.

I'm shoved against the wall and his lips are on mine before I can finish that breath. He quickly releases my wrist and his hands go to my waist, each hand digging into my sides and pulling me closer. His tongue slips past my lips, and I lock my arms around his neck. *Hot damn, this man can kiss.*

Ethan moves his knee between my legs and rubs against me. A moan comes from inside me, fueling his hunger even more. A hand slips under my shirt, snapping me back to attention. I break the kiss.

"Ethan."

"I can't let you go back out there dressed the way you are because I won't be able to keep my eyes or hands off of you. And if I won't be able to do it, no other man out there will either. I don't feel like getting in a fight tonight, Kelsey. It wouldn't be professional and it wouldn't end well for the other guy. I don't know what you've done to me, but I've never felt this way about anyone and I can't get enough of you."

I push him away slightly and look into his eyes. If he really feels this way then where has he been? Why hasn't he called me or come over for breakfast? If he really feels this way, he never would have stopped showing up. But I can't let him know how this bothers me.

"I'm sorry, Ethan, I … I got carried away. I'm not attracted to you that way." I take a step around him.

"That's bullshit, Kelsey, and you know it," he challenges once I reach the door.

"I don't know it. I don't know anything except that a relationship between the two of us would never work."

"Why not? We've never had one. You can't just pre-reject

something because you *think* you know how it will turn out. It doesn't work like that."

I remain silent because everything I say is only making this situation worse. I don't want him upset with me but I do want him to stop being such an uptight jerk.

"I'm sorry, Ethan. I should get back to work."

"Wait. Look me in the eye and tell me you don't having even a pinch of feelings for me. I know you do. I want to hear you say it."

I don't hesitate to look him in the eye. I even open my mouth to confess everything he wants to hear, but the words don't come out. Instead, I open the door and walk out.

Ethan never comes out of his office during my shift. I don't know what is wrong with me, but I do care about him. It's just that after you add our past and his present behavior together, it all screams that I shouldn't trust him. I'm not doing that again. I can't let myself go through that more than once. I know I said I'd just go with it, but I can't. Even if every part of my heart wants to be with Ethan.

CHAPTER SIXTEEN

Kelsey

All week I have failed miserably at hiding my emotions. Both Beth and Logan have threatened that if I don't cheer up by Saturday night, they will call Sara. Calling the best friend can be just as bad as physical pain. Now it's Friday, and Logan and I are once again the bartenders for the night. I'm determined to prove there is nothing wrong with me. Technically there isn't if you take away my obsession with the fact that I think I made a mistake with Ethan. Maybe I should have given us a real chance. Maybe he acted that way because I wasn't ever all that clear on how I felt. I should have gone all in. I was stupid, now I'm miserable.

"Hey, Pip," Logan jokes as he flicks my side ponytail. I laugh, set a few beers on the counter, and start popping off the tops.

"Pip had two pigtails, Logan. I only have one," I correct him, and the customer across from me nods in agreement.

"And Pippy braided her hair too," the man says before taking his beer and walking back to his table.

Logan shakes his head before pulling apart a thirty-pack of beer and squatting to load them into the cooler under the bar top.

"My point is, you're over here bouncing around all cheery and humming along to the music. Lately you're in here all stressed and shit." He stops to look up at me. "Is there something you want to tell me? Has someone finally turned that frown upside down?"

I playfully kick him and he wobbles a little before correcting himself and continues stocking the fridge.

"Nope," I say, giving him a straight face and shrugging my shoulders. "Is there something you should be telling me?"

He stands up and puts his hand on his hips. "You girls are the weirdest creatures, you know that?" I only smile at him. "But you want to know something else?" he adds. "I'm a guy and that makes me smarter than any creature out there, so I know exactly what you're hiding." My smiles drops and he laughs as he walks to other end of the bar.

He's just messing with me. He doesn't know anything—does he? I bet he already talked to Ethan, even though there isn't anything to talk about. Boys are so much worse than girls at gossiping because they don't know when they are doing it. But if they are talking, that means Ethan's been thinking about me. And if he has, maybe all I need to do is talk to him. Fix whatever mess this is. If he were someone I could just get over, I'd have done that by now.

I decide it's best I go about the rest of my shift throwing myself into work. If I'm busy, I won't be able to hear Logan at the other end of the bar making stupid and funny comments about what he thinks he knows, and I sure won't have time to think about Ethan. My plan goes perfectly, but of course, that ends real fast when Ethan walks through the bar door with a girl on his arm. Not just any girl either. He's with Abby.

Ethan

I had a plan and I thought it was brilliant, but looking at Kelsey's face right now, I know I screwed up. I screwed up bad. Abby probably isn't the best person to use for this, but she knew my intentions and said she has no problem helping me out. But the way her hand keeps grabbing my ass, she's created a plan of her own.

"Abby, stop. You're not helping," I tell her as I remove her hand once again. No man in his right mind would say no to a girl when she grabs his ass, so I know I look like a total dumbass right now.

We take a seat at the bar. I watch as Kelsey walks away from us to the other end of the bar where Logan is. He looks over her shoulder at me then nods his head. He hands her the beer bottle in his hand and approaches us.

"Hey, guys," he greets us, but he doesn't sound pleased. We make brief eye contact and then he lets out a deep breath and shakes his head.

"I have to use the ladies' room," Abby says, leaving us.

We both watch as she disappears behind the door.

"Dude, what the fuck are you doing bringing *her* here? I thought you and Kelsey were … I don't know, getting along now or—fuck, you were trying anyway." He keeps shaking his head. "You just messed everything up. I don't know how to help you and I definitely don't want to. Not now. You're on your own."

Logan doesn't have to tell me twice.

"I was desperate. Kelsey won't openly admit she likes me so I thought—"

"That you should make her jealous," he finishes for me. "You don't know her at all, do you? You remember Tyler, right?"

I nod.

"Did you know he cheated on her? With Abby?"

Fuck.

I'm an asshole.

What kind of a person would cheat on Kelsey? Kelsey deserves the best, and I'll hurt anyone who doesn't give that to her, including myself.

"Yeah, I didn't think you knew. And if you did know, this was a complete jackass move."

He hands me a beer and sets some bright cocktail thing in front of Abby's seat, a cranberry vodka maybe—who cares? *I fucked up.*

"Have your drink and get out of here, man. That's the best thing you can do right now. Better yet, just go now," he advises and I nod my head.

The moment Abby returns from the bathroom, we leave. I don't look back to see if Kelsey is watching because I hope to god she isn't.

How am I going to fix this?

CHAPTER SEVENTEEN

Kelsey

The remainder of the evening goes by in a blur because I can't stop thinking about how Abby has ruined something else for me. Logan knew exactly why I asked him to switch sides with me. There was no way I was going to wait on Ethan while he was sitting with *her*. Instead, I just watched them from my end of the bar. I know he was trying to get me to react or at least say something. I wanted to. I wanted to tell Abby she is wasting her time, because he's mine. But all I saw was history repeating itself. *He cheated when he first kissed you, Kelsey. He will do it again.*

I force back the tears as I clear the last table of its empty drinks. Why can't I find a guy who is happy with just one woman? Rain is pouring down outside, and for the last hour, the sound of drops beating against the window is the only thing that has kept me relaxed. I stop, still holding a few dirty glasses, and watch. Everything outside looks cold and depressing, much like my life at this very moment.

I have no one to blame but myself. I can't be upset with anyone but me. Ethan doesn't know about my past relationship. I never told him. I shouldn't be upset with him. We hardly know each other, and one kiss doesn't mean anything.

"Hey, is it cool if I head out?" Logan asks. He pulls on his jacket and pauses at the top of the steps while I head behind the bar.

I set the dishes in the sink and nod my head.

"Of course." I smile at him. He studies me for a minute.

"Is everything alright?"

No.

"Yeah, everything's great. I'm just getting tired," I say, and when he doesn't respond I know he's deciding whether or not to believe me.

"Alright … well, if you need anything, just call, okay?"

"Thanks." I follow behind him as he leaves so I can lock the door.

Before I reach it, the jukebox begins to play "Endless Love" by The Bird and The Bee. *Does everything have to depress me right now?* I used to love this song, but now the words are bound to tear me apart. It's a song that mocks me for something I'll never have. I head for the jukebox with the goal of changing the song to some hate music—because anything would be better than this—when I feel a cold breeze from the front doors opening. I turn to tell whoever it is we're closed, but freeze when I see Ethan standing in the doorway.

He isn't wearing the same clothes as he was earlier, and a pang of dread flows through me as every awful idea runs through my mind. His wet hair drips into his face and his black t-shirt and jeans are sticking to his body. His chest is moving quickly as he breathes and his now dark and determined green eyes are focused on where I stand.

My eyes go wide as I take him in. The wet look makes him even sexier than before, but his eyes are the piece causing me to take a step back. The desire in them matches the exact way my heart feels. He came here for me; I know that much. I also know I'm not letting him leave until we've resolved this one way or another.

Ethan stalks toward me, and when he gets close enough, I take another step behind me, bumping into the pool table. My palms grip the table to steady myself as he presses his body against me and leans forward, placing his hands right next to mine.

"I don't want to play games, Kelsey. I want you and only you. I'm sorry about tonight. Abby doesn't mean anything to me. I have never felt for someone the way I feel about you and I didn't know how to handle it. I still don't, but I do know the only way I want to figure it out is with you. I want you in my life no matter what happens."

I'm stunned speechless. Everything is a clouded mess inside my head. I want to tell him that I want him, too, and together we could have it all, but I can't form words. *Say yes, Kelsey. Say anything. Forget the past.* I manage a small nod.

He doesn't waste any time waiting for more of a response. His lips crash against mine and I wrap my arms around his neck to pull him closer. Our mouths move desperately against one another while his hands glide down my back until he's cupping my butt. He grips each cheek tightly, picking me up and setting me on the table.

"God, I want you so bad," he breathes into my mouth.

My knees part as he moves between them, jerking my

body into his. Since I'm wearing a skirt there isn't much of a barrier left between us, and when he grinds his hips into my core, I can feel how much he wants me and that only fuels my body even more.

"Kelsey," he says, separating our lips and trailing kisses down my neck. I love the way he says my name. I lean my head back to give him better access. Pleased sounds escape my lips as he moves further down my body. His hands find the hem of my shirt and a wave of desire washes through me as they rise underneath it, his fingers reaching the edge of my bra.

The soft music in the background and our rapid breaths surround me. It only intensifies the fire between us. Ethan removes his hands, but I grab his wrist in protest. He smiles and lets out a small laugh. "Trust me, ok?"

I lock my eyes on his, accepting his silent promise, and let go of him. He quickly lifts my shirt over my head. He drops the shirt to the ground and leans back.

"You're so beautiful," he says then kisses me again. He unsnaps my bra, removing it from my body, but never pulls his lips away from mine. His hands find my breasts and he squeezes them gently, letting his thumbs play with my nipples a little longer.

I moan into his mouth and the warmth between my legs tells me how much I enjoy what he does to me. I let my hands roam over his body slowly and stop at the waist of his jeans. My fingers unbuckle them and once I have them unzipped, I slide my hands underneath and around to his backside. I put my hands flat against his firm body and pull him into me, moving my waist against him as I hold him there.

"Ah fuck," he cries, quickly moving his hands to my skirt. "I can't wait much longer."

With his admission we take full advantage of removing every last piece of clothing from the other's body. Once I'm completely naked, he picks me up to move me back to the middle of the table and then he climbs up to join me, crawling over me until his body is above mine. *We're totally going to have sex on top of a pool table.* This isn't like me, but I love it.

Ethan gently lowers himself between my legs. The feel of his skin brushing against mine sets my body off. I want him to touch me anywhere his hands will go. His lips trail kisses across my cheek, down my neck, and between my breasts.

"God, you smell like cinnamon," he says, pulling my nipple into his mouth and sucking hard. My hips lift of the table at the sensation his lips send through my body. I moan, causing Ethan to grab my waist. He holds it firm against his. Moving from one breast to the other, his hands glide to the back of my thighs, to the inside of them, climbing higher until I almost lose myself the moment his fingers touch my core. Slowing, he slides one in, then another. He keeps kissing me and with each stroke I'm more turned on. I don't want to wait anymore. I want him inside me.

I pull my body away quickly, taking him off guard as I push him on his back. With one leg on each side of him, I gaze down at his body.

"You are so fucking hot."

"Kelsey, don't swear or I'm going to lose my shit."

I smile and kiss him hard. His hands move to my waist, positioning me right over him and slowly, I lower myself on to him.

"Fuck," he growls, grabbing my face and refusing to let our lips part.

I grind my hips, his meeting mine thrust for thrust. Each movement is perfect, rough, and when he stills my body, I try my hardest to continue. I pull my lips from his to look him in the eye.

"Don't move," he breathes. "Just stay right there."

I do as I'm told and in seconds, Ethan is ramming his hips up harder and faster. My head falls back as I let out sounds I didn't know I could make.

Two more thrusts and we both fall into a bliss I never knew existed. From this moment on, I have a feeling Ethan is about to show me a lot of things I didn't know.

Ethan

We're still lying on the pool table after our bodies relax. I have Kelsey firmly secured in my arms. I hadn't planned this. *Liar.* Alright, so it was a possibility in the back of my mind, but I didn't make her do anything she didn't want to do.

Bringing Abby here tonight was a mistake, but I'm not upset with the way the evening turned out. Had I not messed up and then turned so desperate I couldn't wait to see Kelsey again, I wouldn't be here right now.

I pull Kelsey's body closer to mine, her back to my front, and I trail soft kisses across her shoulders. I spot three freckles just under her left ear and kiss each of them. Ever since our first kiss, I knew there was something between us that I would never find with someone else. We might have only been teenagers, but when you know, you know. I ruined it then, but I'm not going to ruin it now. I'm going to tell her everything. I just need to find the right time to do it.

"We should probably get dressed," Kelsey suggests, but I don't want to move.

"Let's just lay here a while longer," I tell her and she laughs as I pinch her sides playfully.

"Ethan, anyone could walk by the windows and see us if they look close enough. I don't feel like giving a free show."

I hadn't thought of that. I don't want anyone to see what's mine. I quickly move off the table, pulling Kelsey with me, and then I stand between her and the window as she gets dressed.

"Hmm, I'd say by the way you're watching me, I should probably keep my clothes off," she teases as she pulls on her shirt and stands in front of me fully clothed.

My body reacts to her words. She's right. I'm ready to do it all over again. She bends down to grab my boxers and jeans then tosses them to me with a big smile on her face.

"If you help me finish closing this place down, we could go back your place, maybe watch a movie," she says, already pushing chairs into the tables. I observe her perfect body from the backside as she walks away.

I better not screw this up.

CHAPTER EIGHTEEN

Kelsey

There's no easy way to say it. I, Kelsey Brian, am that girl, that girl who sleeps with her boss. *Oh. My. God.* I can't stop thinking about last night. I'll never be able to look at the pool table the same again, or the whole bar for that matter.

That's not even the worst part. The worst part is I went back to his house to do it again. And I want it even more now than I did last night. Not in the bar of course. Although, I don't think I would object to it if the situation were right. I mean, who doesn't enjoy a little excitement from a place where you could get caught? *Oh shit.* What if someone actually did see us through the window?

"Kelsey, dude … you're freaking me out."

I blink myself back to the present at the sound of Logan's voice. He's standing right in front of me with his hands on my shoulders, squatting down to meet me at eye level.

"Huh?"

"You look like you've seen a ghost, and you were focused on the pool table like you were trying to make it float or something," he says, removing his hands and waving them in the air. "All you needed was the snap of your fingers or a wand or some shit."

He takes a step back, shaking his head as he laughs.

"Man, would I love to know what's going on it that head of yours."

No. No you would not.

I let out a deep breath and turn around to fill a couple of beer buckets with ice.

"It wasn't anything important."

"Yeah, okay," he says with disbelief.

"Hey, Kelsey, do you have those beers ready? My table is getting antsy," Beth says as she pretty much bounces her way to the end of the bar. She bats her eyelashes at Logan.

"Hey, Logan," she says in a flirty tone. He looks at me then glances at Beth.

"How's it going, Beth?" I know him well enough to know he is just trying to be polite, but that he also doesn't really want to talk to her. It's the tone he uses when he isn't in the mood to talk to anyone. He's been in a bad mood ever since he got off the phone with Sara earlier today.

"It's going," she says. "Are you working late tonight?"

Logan lets out a long sigh. He looks up at the same time Abby appears.

"Hey, Logan." She smiles flirtatiously. "Want to get a drink after work tonight?"

Well, this just got awkward and interesting. I set Beth's beer bucket on the counter and then lean my hip against it and cross my arms as I watch.

"Uhhh,"

"Shit, Ethan's here," Beth announces, cutting Logan off before he can say anything.

Ethan in blue jeans and a button-down shirt will never get old. There is an unfamiliar smile on his face as he comes down the steps. His grin grows bigger when his eyes land on me. I can feel my cheeks beginning to heat up.

"Crap! He sees us," Abby whines and both she and Beth quickly scatter from the bar.

"Well, that's one way to solve my problem. Guess Ethan is good for something after all." Logan laughs and strolls to the other end of the bar as a couple of customers pull up a stool. I give him a look that I intend to scream "no, don't leave me alone" as he walks away, but he shrugs his shoulders and nods his head in Ethan's direction.

The whole place feels like a sauna and I'm convinced someone keeps turning up the heat. Ethan walks past the pool table, running his fingers along the felt. Flashes of last night cloud my mind. I focus on my breathing, and by the time Ethan reaches me, I think I've pulled it together.

"Hey, Kelsey," he says in a tone I haven't heard before. He sounds—calm, happy maybe. It relaxes and excites me all at the same time. I grab a towel to wipe the counter between us.

"Hey, Ethan." I can't even look at him without getting images of last night. This isn't good *at all*. He starts to drum his fingers against the bar top, and as I steal a quick glance I notice they are shaking slightly. How could he be nervous after last night? He sure wasn't nervous then. His hands didn't shake when he touched me, while they explored every inch of my body.

"Look … I … ugh," he whispers. "I wanted to … um …" As he tries to find his words, he is staring down at his left hand and the right is behind his neck. "Last night was …"

Oh my god, if he finishes that sentence with the word *mistake*, I could possibly lose my job when I lunge my body over this counter and kill him.

"Well I … I was hoping I could take you on a date."

That is not what I was expecting. His gaze rises and I stare into his bright green eyes. There's a different sparkle to them,

"A date?" I repeat.

"Yeah, I know it's a little backward considering our track record, but I want to take you out. Last night was … perfect." He sounds more confident this time.

"What happened last night?" Logan asks and I jump when I realize how close he's standing. Does this guy ever work, or is he always lingering—and how much did he hear?

"Nothing," I answer automatically before stepping around Logan to attend the customers at the other end of the bar. It's Saturday and the night is starting slow. I ask the three people seated in stools if they need anything, but they kindly decline. *So much for that distraction.*

I try to busy myself by organizing the liquor bottles, washing all the dirty glasses—there aren't many since we switch to plastic after five—and wiping down the counters. Once I have cleaned everything else I can see, there's nothing left to distract me.

I could go on a date with Ethan. It makes total sense for a new couple, but it's completely inappropriate considering he's my boss. I know I thought differently last night, but I was caught up in the moment and I can't let that interfere with the right thing to do. I let out a sigh of frustration and lean forward on the bar. On the other hand, if I say no to him again, I could really mess things up. Which matters more, falling in love or keeping my job? Sara wouldn't fire me, but if Ethan and I didn't work out, would he?

My moment of silence is interrupted when I hear a group near the jukebox break out in laughter, gaining the attention of the entire bar. They fall silent, focusing their attention on someone nearby. I can't hear what they are saying, but soon the group is laughing again. A woman scoots her chair back and stands slowly before heading for the bathroom. I have a clear view of the comedian and I'm shocked to see it's Ethan.

"He seems awfully happy tonight." Logan startles me, but I don't even glance up. If I make even the slightest expression, he will know what it means before I do.

"Yeah, looks that way."

"Wouldn't have anything to do with last night, would it?" he asks.

Ethan told him. *No, no, no.* Logan will tell Sara.

"Please, please don't tell Sara. She will kill me." I start to ramble cupping my hands together as I beg. "I was just closing the bar. He came back to talk and then it got out of hand and before I knew it, it was too late and we couldn't take it back."

Logan finally looks up with a puzzled expression.

"Take what back?" A half smile tugs at his lips.

Giant crap! I just spilled the beans.

Logan watches me for a minute then glances at Ethan, who's still near the same group of people, only now he is leaning against the pool table and staring down at it with a huge grin on his face. *Aw, damn.* Dead giveaway.

Now Logan's eyes spring wide. He fails miserably at trying to hide the full smile on his face.

"No fucking way! Oh man, tell me you didn't!" I just stand there. I was never quick in these situations and I have no idea what to say, so I just scrunch my face.

He slams his hand on the counter and I jump.

"Hot damn, Sara is going to love this." He chuckles and reaches to his back pocket to pull out his cellphone. I reach for it as quickly as I can, but he pulls back.

"Please don't tell Sara! I'm begging you, Logan."

"Tell Sara what?" Ethan asks as he pulls up a stool across from us. *Geez!* Doesn't anyone keep to themselves around here?

"Nothing," I say and give Logan my best threatening look. "Right, Logan?"

"Right, Kelsey," he nods.

The three of us stand there looking at each other—me worried, Logan with a grin, and Ethan confused.

Maybe now isn't the best time to give Ethan my answer. No audience would be best.

Ethan

After Kelsey went home last night, I laid awake—something I've done a lot since I met her—for hours imaging what it would be like to not give a shit about my dad. About whether or not he's proud of me. I wouldn't have to snoop around the bar anymore, I wouldn't have to lie to anyone, and I sure as shit could have something real with Kelsey.

Before I fell asleep, I knew I'd made up my mind. He can

send one of my brothers, but I'm not letting them anywhere near the bar or near Kelsey. I'm going to get to know her better and I'm going to start with a date. But it isn't working out how I planned, because now she's avoiding my question.

"So, Ethan," Logan crosses his arms. He nods to the pool table with his head. "Something wrong with the felt?" Kelsey looks terrified. "You didn't get anything on it, did you? By accident of course." He laughs and walks away.

It's hard not to laugh with him. Logan is smart and he put two and two together. But he was only messing with her.

Kelsey stands with her hands locked behind her back and stares down at her feet. How can she be nervous after what we did last night? Is she embarrassed like she was when I kissed her all those years ago?

"I meant everything I told you last night. I want to give us a real shot," I say.

Her cheeks turn a soft shade of pink and she nods.

"Okay. Let's go on a date then."

"Tomorrow night. I'll pick you up at six."

"I work tomorrow."

"Not anymore." I give her a wink.

"You can't just change the schedule like that, Ethan. It's not fair to anyone else who works here."

"I can if I want. I haven't been this happy since I came here—you can ask anyone here and I guarantee, if it puts me in a better mood, they'd be more than willing to work for you tomorrow night."

I look over my shoulder for Beth or Abby. Either of them would love to help. Lucky for me, Beth is headed our way and I know she isn't on the schedule for tomorrow.

"Beth, want to work tomorrow night?" I ask.

She pauses, her eyes flickering between Kelsey and me. "Is this a trick question?"

"Don't listen to him, Beth. He's still learning how to manage this place," Kelsey says with a cheery tone.

Beth's eyes go wide as she presses her lips together.

"I'm actually doing just fine, Kelsey, thank you." I give her a playful grin. "I asked Kelsey out on a date, but she's working and needs someone to cover her shift."

"Wait, so like, you'd be gone too?" Beth asks.

I nod.

"Yeah, sure, I'll totally work for you, Kelsey."

I ignore the excitement in her voice and instead focus on Kelsey. It goes without question that she makes me want to be a better person and her presence always puts me in a good mood. I am determined to make this dinner perfect.

I flash Kelsey one last grin and catch the sight of her smile before I head for the office.

I close the door as my cellphone vibrates inside my pants pocket. All the happiness I'm feeling fades when I see my father's name on the phone.

"Sir," I answer and take a seat behind the desk.

"You haven't called me with an update. I can't decide whether or not that means things are going in my favor or if you're not getting the job done. Your behavior is really starting to piss me off, and you're about out of second chances." His criticizing voice is firm. His mind is already made up. He just wants to test me.

"I still haven't found anything that will lead me to the account numbers you want, but I think I'm on to something. I just need a little more time," I lie to him. If I convince him to believe me, I can buy more time until I tell Kelsey what's been going on. A first date isn't the right time to drop this sort of information. A few days are all I need. She'll believe me and trust me. I know she will.

CHAPTER NINETEEN

Ethan

I really don't have to pick Kelsey up considering she's right across the street, but I pull my bike into her driveway anyway and swing my leg over, a bouquet full of lilies in my hand. My nerves are running through my body in a hurry. I stop in front of her door, attempting to collect myself. I hold the flowers tightly as I smooth out the nonexistent wrinkles on my light blue button-down shirt.

I can do this. It's no different than anyone else. Except, it is different. This means something. Kelsey means something.

I knock twice on the door and she opens it right away as if she were waiting on the other side.

"Hi." She smiles at me and I'm at a loss for words. She's breathtaking. "Are those for me?" She points to the flowers in my hand.

"Yes," I say, almost shoving them in her face.

"Come in," she says, stepping inside. "I just need to put them in water before we go."

I wait in the doorway.

"You don't have to just stand there," she hollers, and I hear her laugh fade as she steps into the kitchen.

Kelsey reaches for a vase on the top shelf of a cabinet, the same one from the first time I bought her flowers. Her arms are stretched high and she's on her tiptoes. Her shirt hangs just above her hip, giving me a glimpse of her smooth skin.

"Do you think you could reach this for me?" she asks, her head cocked to the side. I step around the counter, reaching for the vase and never taking my eyes off of her. I grab it, setting it on the counter.

"Here," I say, but she just stares at me. Her hand touches my chest and she curls her fingers against it. Then she pulls me in and kisses me.

I kiss her back, grabbing her hips and moving her between me and the counter. I pin her there as I bring our bodies closer together. Her tongue slips into my mouth, and she deepens the kiss. At this rate, we'll never make it to dinner.

"We should probably get going," she says between kisses, and I regrettably step away. She puts the flowers in water, and I take her hand, pulling her next to me as we walk to my bike. "We're not seriously riding that, are we?" she asks with a panicked look on her face.

"We are. Is this okay?"

"Yeah, I just—I've never been on the back of one of these before," she says, and I catch the small blush that fills her cheeks. I hand her a helmet and then help her put it on before doing the same for myself.

"Just hold on tight," I say as I back the bike out of her driveway.

I made plans for us to go to Italios Pasta House for dinner

and then walk downtown and talk. I'm following Sara's advice to get to know her. It's a little late, but we're going to have plenty of time together to make up for that. I haven't told Kelsey any of this, but I have a feeling she will enjoy it.

"Don't you want to know where I'm taking you for our date?" I ask.

"Nope. I trust you." She says it like it's that simple. If she only knew what I came here to do for my father. I would lose her trust the moment I earned it.

I start the bike, its engine roaring as we pull out of the driveway. The last girl I had on my bike tried to talk the entire time. It was hard to hear her, and by the time we got off she was mad and claimed I was ignoring her. With Kelsey it's nothing but peaceful. Her arms wrap around me and her chest rests against my back. Everything with Kelsey is easy and feels perfect.

I pull into the parking lot and hear her clapping behind me. When I glance back she has a giant grin on her face.

"How did you know this was my favorite place?"

I shrug and turn off the engine. "When I would visit in the summers, we always came here for your birthday."

"You remember that?"

"I remember everything. Even the part where I was only invited because Sara's mom made her invite me." I laugh. "But I was happy either way. I got to see you. That was the only reason I kept coming back."

"Oh," she says and looks away as her cheeks turn a light shade of pink. She blushes more than anyone I know, but she looks damn adorable every time.

I hold the bike steady as she gets off and then I hold her

hand as we walk inside. The smell of pasta and fresh bread fill the restaurant and my stomach growls.

"Two?" the young boy behind the wooden stand asks.

"Yes. It should be under Connelly."

The boy scans the paper in front of him with his index finger and then taps it against the stand. "Yep. Please follow me."

I place my hand at the small of Kelsey's back as we follow the kid. He shows us to a corner booth and sets the menus down, leaving us alone. Kelsey scoots inside the booth and I scoot in right next to her.

"It's smells so good in here," she says.

"Yeah, I'm starving," I reply, opening a menu. "Are you going to order the four cheese stuffed ravioli in Alfredo sauce?"

She smiles at me, nods, and looks back to her menu. "I can't believe you remember that. I was impressed enough that you remembered my favorite restaurant."

"I probably remember a lot more than you think."

"Hmm, okay, name three things," she challenges me in a flirty tone.

"Only three?"

"Yep." She wiggles three fingers in the air.

"Alright, I remember how every Fourth of July you were crazy into those red, white, blue firecracker popsicles. I swear you ate one every day for a month every summer."

She laughs but nods.

"When Sara's parents would throw her birthday barbeque, you spent more time helping her mother make sure everything was ready than hanging out with your girlfriends. Making other people happy made you happy. You've always been selfless like that and it's a beautiful trait to have."

Her eyes meet mine, but she doesn't say anything.

"And I also remember when I kissed you behind Sara's house that day—from that moment on I knew you would always be special to me."

A gloss takes over her golden eyes, causing them to shine bright. She leans over and gently presses her lips to mine.

The waiter clears his throat and Kelsey pulls away. She blushes but doesn't try to hide it the way she does every other time it happens. He takes our drink order, leaving us alone again, and like love-struck fools, we just smile at each other.

I'm nailing this date thing. Being with Kelsey is so easy, and if I can get her to smile that way every time she sees me, I'll be one happy man.

Kelsey

Our date is going amazingly. The food was great, but the company is the best I could've asked for. We finished eating about an hour ago, but we've been sitting here talking about the things we've missed over the years.

I told him about my parents and their dream to travel. I told him about my little brother who left the day after he graduated and whom I've only spoken with on the phone since that day. I told him about school and all the pointless details that got me to where I am now. I don't tell him about my ex, because during those summers Ethan visited, Tyler was his friend. I don't want to ruin things if they still are. Still, I feel as though we're far enough into the conversation I can ask him the one question I've been dying to know.

"Your dad owns a lot of his own businesses, so why did you come to the BA instead of working for him?"

Ethan plays with the fork still left on the table as he debates his answer.

"He never offered me a spot to work with him." His voice is low, and from the way his face wrinkles as he says it, I can tell it's something that bothers him. "I thought if I could come here and things went … as planned, he would be proud and maybe change his mind."

His last words hit close to home. I'm an accounting major only to get my father's attention, but I'm not letting that take over. I'm still writing and I'm applying for jobs that involve writing. But something in his voice alarms me. Like he's letting his father decide how things will turn out for him instead of making that decision on his own.

"Have you talked to him about it?" I ask, hesitantly.

"No. Have you talked to your dad about what bothers you?"

I shake my head. "We may not see eye to eye, and he isn't very active in my life, but I know he loves me and one day things will be different."

"Yeah, I don't think my dad will ever change. My mom's been trying to change him for years, and the man won't budge. He's got a one-track mind. His way or no way."

My heart breaks a little seeing this vulnerable side to Ethan. I want to change the subject because I don't like him being upset, but I want him to know he can talk to me about these sort of things.

"Maybe—"

"How about we talk about something else?" he says in a

much cheerier tone. "My family drama isn't going to ruin the rest of the night."

"Okay, but you can always—"

"I know." He cuts me off and kisses my temple. "And thank you, but another night would be better."

After Ethan pays the bill, he slowly laces his fingers with mine as I rise from my seat. In that moment the very person I wanted to avoid tonight walks past our table. Tyler. He stops in front of us, shock written all over his face. His gaze bounces back and forth between us.

"Ethan, I thought you were going to hit me up when you had a night off." Tyler offers his hand, and Ethan accepts it with a quick, firm shake that makes Tyler cringe. "We could grab a drink now; my dad would probably enjoy catching up with you too."

"I'd love that," Officer Maron says, walking up behind Tyler. "Kelsey, it's great to see you again."

"Whoa, man, strong grip," Tyler says, prying his hand away from Ethan. I hadn't even realized they were still shaking hands. *Weird.*

"We were just leaving," Ethan says. "Maybe next time."

He rushes us to his bike, giving me my helmet before putting his on, too, and quickly pulls out the parking lot heading for home. Our date just went from good to bad in seconds, and now Tyler's responsible for ruining something else that I wanted.

Ethan pulls the bike into his driveway and just sits there. The September air is growing colder, and Ethan probably won't be able to ride his bike much longer. His mood has taken a complete 180 since we left the restaurant. After Logan told me how much this bike means to Ethan, I sit on the back, not rushing him.

"I'm sorry about that. I wanted to beat his face in, no questions asked." He lets out a breath. "Logan told me what Tyler did and with who … I swear I didn't know, and if I had I would have never shown up with her. I swear."

"Ethan, stop, everything is fine." I lift my leg over the bike, handing him my helmet so I can stand and face him. "Everyone makes mistakes—it's how you handle them that defines who you are. Besides, we weren't dating then, so I don't really have a reason to be mad."

"Still, I should have just asked why you couldn't be with me before you caved and told me. It was a dick move."

"Yeah, but at least you know it, and if Tyler hadn't cheated on me, I wouldn't be here right now, with you," I flirt with him, noting the exact moment he relaxes. "So technically, we should thank Tyler for getting us here."

He kicks the stand on the bike as he gets up. The look in his eyes twists my stomach as I lean forward over the bike. His lips press against mine.

"Did you say we were dating now?" he asks, pulling away only until the words are out. He kisses me again, but before I can answer, the sound of screeching tires skidding to a stop makes me jump back.

A truck the exact image of Ethan's, only black, parks in front of his house. The dome light comes on at the same time Ethan whispers "fuck" behind me. I watch as the light fades and the driver's door closes after someone gets out. Then a man, probably a few years older than Ethan, steps around the truck.

"Baby brother." The man smiles coyly. "Looks like I'm crashing with you for a few days."

Ethan groans and rubs his hands over his face. That's not the reaction I would have if my brother showed up. I'd be thrilled and even hug him. Ethan might not be a hugging person, but he sure doesn't look happy.

"Hey there," the blonde man says to me. He reaches his hand out. "I'm Lance."

I shake his hand. "Hi."

He chuckles. "And you are?"

"I'm—"

"Leaving." Ethan cuts in, walking around his bike to nudge me toward my house. "I'll call you tomorrow. We can talk about that shift change then."

What the—?

"Please," he whispers so only I can hear him. His eyes are pleading as he darts them between me and his brother.

I get that he might not want his family to know he has something going on with me just yet, but it still stings that he is referring to me as just an employee right now. At least he could have told his brother I was a friend or a neighbor. Either way, this reaction is bullshit.

"Yeah, sure thing." The sentence is nothing but sarcasm, and from the worried expression Ethan just gave me, he knows he just ruined our first date.

I walk away hearing a faint "she's feisty" from his brother. I'd really like to turn around and flip him the bird, but I can be more mature about this. Instead, with all this run of new emotion I have, I think I'll work on my essay. The life of a twenty-something girl and her failed attempts to make a relationship work with the same guy might make for interesting story. In fact, since this is going to be a column about my personal life, this would be a great opening piece and might just be the one to win me this job.

CHAPTER TWENTY

Kelsey

I wrote the entire essay in two hours last night. Edited it first thing this morning and now I'm confidently handing it in.

"You're really going to enter that? I didn't realize you wanted to be a writer that badly," Logan comments once I've returned to my seat. Professor Frank announced today was an in-class writing day, so everyone is sitting quietly at their seats, scribbling notes. Everyone except Logan because he doesn't like to write. I glance at his paper; hangman is all it shows. I laugh to myself, shaking my head.

"Like most of the other people in this class, I happen to enjoy writing."

"But to do it every day?" He sounds doubtful.

"Twenty-four hours a day," I assure him. "I'd love it."

"Okay, why writing? Why not art?"

"Because I suck at art and writing just comes to me. I can have all these conversations in my head and assign them to different characters. I can give them lives I'll never live.

Fancier or maybe more exciting lives. It's nothing different than a movie. I just leave mine on paper instead of making it into a film." Not very many people ask me why I write anymore. It's nice to know some people don't just think I'm weird.

"So you write about the life you want?"

"No, that would be crazy and in some cases really disturbing."

"Interesting," he says, drawing up another hangman game. "So what's up with you and Ethan?" Now I know why he was acting overly interested—he was building to this.

"Nothing." I shrug.

"Lies. Come on, tell me." His voice is nearing the begging side and that's when it clicks.

"Sara asked you to ask me that, didn't she?"

"Nope." He shakes his head. "She did not."

"Yeah, okay, we're not really anything. I don't think Ethan knows what he wants."

"Why do you say that?" Logan asks.

"Okay everyone! Let's end class here. If you haven't turned your entry in for the columnist spot, you have exactly twenty seconds to do so or you're out."

I glance around to see who my competition might be, but no one steps up. I saw three other papers on the prof's desk so I know I'm not alone, and he has more than one class, but the fewer who enter, the better. My paper is going to grab their attention, I just know it.

"Hey." Logan taps my desk. "Let's go and you can tell me your Ethan theory."

I follow him out of the room with the other students.

"He was just acting weird last night after his brother showed up. He couldn't even introduce me to him," I say.

Logan nods, pushing to doors open to step outside.

"It's like one minute he likes me, the next he has no idea. I don't get it."

"Well, you better figure it out quick because confused lover boy is standing by your car."

I stop, looking directly at Ethan. He's got a bouquet of flowers in his hand and a nervous look on his face. This would be much easier if he could look happy all the time instead of like someone who keeps messing up. Or he could just stop messing up. I stroll toward him, crossing my arms over my chest. Whatever his excuse is this time, it better be good because I swear, one more chance is all this guy is going to get.

Ethan

I fucked up, again. At this point I should stop trying and just leave the girl alone, but I can't. I've never found someone whose opinion meant more to me than my father's and I'm not about to let her go that easily.

As she hesitantly approaches, I cringe inside at the reminder of how I put us into this spot.

I should have introduced her as my girlfriend. Anything would have been better than placing her into the employee category. I'm an idiot.

"Hey," I say when she stops in front of me. I'm leaning against the hood of her car. I had this whole speech planned out. One where I confess, *again*, to what a jackass I am and how I won't let it happen *again*. But now I can't think of anything except just being near her.

Her eyebrow rises as she crosses her arms over her books in front of her.

"Do you think we can talk?" I ask. Kelsey huffs and her car chirps behind me once she's hit the unlock button.

"No, you had time to talk last night, but instead you didn't. Actually, that's a lie. You said plenty when you made it clear to your brother that I was just an employee."

She tries to nudge me away, but I don't budge.

"I was caught off guard. I didn't want my family to think I came down here to get managing experience only to start hooking up with someone who works there."

"Well, you did."

"Yeah, but not in the way it sounds."

"That doesn't even make sense, Ethan. If that's not what happened between us, then what was it? We hooked up. It was fun. That's the end of it."

She jerks her car door hard, smacking me with it. I step back and grab the frame.

"I like you, Kelsey. It was more than just a hookup to me," I finally admit. I don't sound very manly, but sometimes the truth isn't.

Kelsey laughs sarcastically. "Well, I'd hate to see how you treat the girl you fall in love with."

"Just give me one more chance, Kelsey. I swear to you this time. I will not mess it up."

"Ethan—"

I don't let her finish the rejection that is on her lips. Instead, I crash mine against them. Her body freezes for a moment before her mouth responds. I grab the books out of her hand and toss them in the car.

This right here, the passion and the way I care about nothing but her, this is why I can't stay away and it's the exact reason why I have to get this right.

"This is your last chance," she says. "I mean it, Ethan. I'm an idiot to give it to you, so do not make me look like a fool."

I step back, holding her door until she slides inside her car.

"I won't, you can trust me."

Even as I say the words, I know they are just as much to convince myself as they are her. Now all I need to do is find the perfect time to explain further why I'm here and not working for my father.

* * *

"You sure ran off in a hurry this morning," Lance says when I walk through my front door. I head for the kitchen and he follows me.

He didn't ask me any questions last night. Nothing about Kelsey or the bar. Sometimes I wonder if he really cares what happens or not. He doesn't seem too concerned about running the BA or being an accomplice to expanding the family feud going on between Sara's dad and ours. Yet he's still here, just like my father said he would be.

"I didn't realize I had to inform you of my schedule."

"Dad seems to think you do."

"Dad has a control problem."

Lance glances at me with a shocked expression. I stare back at him, ready for whatever defense he decides to throw my way, but it never comes. Instead, he chuckles as he takes bottled water from the fridge.

"You're probably the first brother to admit that out loud." He takes a drink. "And you're damn lucky you said it to me— Ben might kick your ass."

"What do you want?" I take a seat at the table. "Uncle Dean doesn't have anything for me to find. They keep everything clean. There's no way Dad could pull this off."

"So tell him that," Lance says, sitting across from me. "Tell him you can't find anything and go home."

"I can't."

"Why not?"

"Because I made a commitment to Sara. I can't abandon the bar while she's gone."

"Ethan, Dean will be able to handle it just fine."

I shake my head.

"He's not here. He's off searching for a new building so he can make the bar into a chain. That's why they called Dad in the first place."

"So there isn't any reason for you to stay. Not even that girl across the street."

My teeth grind as I look him in the eyes. "Stay away from Kelsey."

He laughs. "Okay, so wait a second. Let me see if I have this right. For years, you've wanted Dad to know he can depend on you, begging him for the chance to prove it to him, so he sends you here. Then, all of the sudden, an account number is hard to find. You think he's controlling, and now you're growling at me with an 'I'll beat your ass' look because I mentioned a girl. What happened when you got here?"

I blink a few times as I think about it.

"I guess all I needed was a life without him in it to figure out what kind of person I am."

Lance nods but doesn't say anything. A half grin appears on his face as he stands.

"I think I'd better head out. Dad clearly underestimated you, as did I. I thought you'd stay his puppet forever. I'm proud of you."

He heads for the door and I watch him, still processing the fact he didn't come here to sabotage me.

"If Dad calls, let's pretend I'm still here taking over for you. I need some time away myself, and you seem to have your shit under control."

And just like that, he leaves.

One obstacle down and one left to go. All I have to do is build Kelsey's trust back up and my life will be smooth sailing and secret free.

CHAPTER TWENTY-ONE

Kelsey

"Gross, you two make me want to vomit." Beth's whines from across the table, make me blush. "Can't I eat my lunch without having to witness people sticking their tongues down each other's throat?" She guards her eyes with her hands.

"Oh, come on, Beth. When you find someone you're head over heels for, you will understand." Logan said.

"Seriously, Logan, you're defending them?"

"Yeah, why not?"

"You're not even dating anyone."

"But he could be …" Ethan chimes in and nods at Logan. "Right?"

"Yep, that's right."

"Whatever. All I'm saying is that I've seen this every night I've worked at the bar for the last month and a half. Haven't you moved past this stage yet?" Beth asks.

I grin toward Ethan, who mimics my expression. She's right. You would think we would be out of this phase, but we're not even close. My father would be furious if he knew I've spent more nights at Ethan's than guarding his house. I don't mind it one bit. Waking up with Ethan has been amazing.

Class has been even better. I got the letter this morning about being a finalist in the column competition. Some people from the paper want to meet with me for a dinner in couple weeks, right before Thanksgiving, where they will end the night announcing the winner. It's like my entire life has finally become what I've wanted. I know it sounds lame and cliché that I could feel this way so soon, but I've never been happier.

I look forward to the days when Ethan meets us all at the college cafeteria for lunch, like today. Beth usually doesn't join us, and although I like when she does, I'm guessing she won't much longer.

"Okay, well I better run. Someone has to open the bar." Ethan stands and then leans down to kiss me one more time. I slip my tongue into his mouth, and he rests his hand on the table to deepen the kiss before leaving for the BA.

"Okay … now I'm taking Beth's side." Logan laughs and waves to Ethan when he leaves. "Have you talked to Sara recently?"

"Yes, every morning. Why?"

Logan's head snaps up and hurt washes over his face. "She hasn't been answering my calls."

Shoot, that's not good.

"I'm sure she's just busy. She's having the time of her life, you know. I bet …" The scent of tuna fish floats through the air and I gag. "I bet …" I get another whiff and I barely get my hand over my mouth as my lunch starts to come back up. I dash from the table to the closest trash can.

"Hey, are you okay?" A hand begins to rub my shoulder and then I see a water bottle lower into my vision. I grab it, swish some water around in my mouth, spit it out, and take a seat at the nearest table. Thank god there aren't many people in here; that was not something anyone wants to see.

"I'm fine." I say, giving Logan a weak smile before gathering my things and heading home. Now is not the time to catch the flu, because that's all it could be. I've repeated that sentence every day since I started throwing up, and I'm praying I'm right. A nap before work should cure whatever I am coming down with. When I get to work tonight, all I have to tell Ethan is that I have a real shot at this job. That's it. I won't have anything else to tell him and the next couple weeks will fly by just as planned until they announce the winner.

And that winner is going to be me because nothing is going to mess up any more of my plans. Nothing.

Both the columnist dinner and Thanksgiving are just days away. Logan and I slowly make our way down the steps after class lets out for break. The weather has been getting colder and the snow has been nonstop. Ethan is leaning against my car. His cheeks are rosy, and he's wearing a red hoodie and dark blue jeans with his legs crossed at the ankles while he plays on his cellphone. He looks sexy as always, and I still can't believe he's mine.

"Hey, gorgeous," Ethan greets me pulling me in for a hug and burying his face in my neck. I don't say anything back, because if I do, I'll say the wrong thing and start crying and then he'll ask questions. Questions I'm not ready to answer. He trails kisses from my ear until he reaches my mouth. I kiss him back and wrap my arms around his neck. I love these moments, when nothing matters but him and me.

I'm going to ruin everything.

"Dude, really, we're standing in a parking lot. Save it for later. It was cute a month ago but now, it's just—just stop," Logan complains, but deep down I know he doesn't care. I think he's still having problems reaching Sara, but I'm not sure how to bring it up. Ethan pulls away, but not before he gives me a few more quick kisses.

"I'd love to stay and continue this, but Logan and I have plans," he says, sticking out his bottom lip and then placing a kiss on my forehead.

"Dude, we're going to play ball, so you better man the fuck up before we get there. Let's go," Logan says, pulling Ethan by his shirt.

"I'll call you later!" he shouts as he climbs into his truck, where Logan waits impatiently in the passenger seat, watching me through the window. I've been getting sick a lot in class lately, and I threw up twice today. After the second time, he kept looking at me all weird. I avoided making any eye contact with him until class was over, but it was almost like he could read my mind.

I think I'm pregnant.

I drive straight to Sara's and my apartment. If I remember right, we already have a test there that I can take. This isn't the first time one of us has been in this situation. I just hope it turns out the same as the other times. I run up the stairs and dash straight for the bathroom, but that door is locked. How is it locked? No one's even living here.

"Just a minute," a female voice calls from inside. The waterworks flow instantly at her voice. I can't imagine a better time for Sara to be home. I need my best friend now more than ever.

She opens the door, smiling, and holds her arms out wide.

"Did you miss—oh my gosh, what's wrong?" Her smile drops and she pulls me in for a hug.

"I think I'm pregnant," I blurt out, but you can hardly understand me over the sobs. If only it was that easy for me to tell Ethan.

"What? How? Who?" She fires the questions at me, but I don't answer as I walk past her to the sink. I dig around in the medicine cabinet, looking for that stupid box.

"I thought we had a test in here," I say, trying to pull myself together. She shuffles her feet, avoiding eye contact.

"I had to use it before I left."

"What! Why didn't you tell me?" What a pair we make. Wait no … scratch that. What an *irresponsible* pair we make.

"It doesn't matter. It was a false alarm. We have more important things to worry about now." She pulls me to my feet, and we leave for the store.

Sara offers to act like it is her test and I let her. *Real mature, Kelsey.* I'm pretty sure the clerk knows the truth though, seeing as I am the one with bloodshot, tear-stained eyes. Sara looks calm as ever. When we get back to the apartment, I rush to the bathroom. I'm so happy Sara is here. She must have had some friend radar telling her that I needed her. It's probably just stress, but once this is over, I'll have to remember to ask her the real reason she's back.

CHAPTER TWENTY-TWO

Kelsey

Positive.

That can't be right.

The purple box I dreaded buying for fear of the results is sitting on the white marble bathroom sink, and when I grab it to re-read the instructions I nearly crumple it into a ball with my grip.

"Minus sign and minus sign means not pregnant, plus sign and minus sign means pregnant." I repeat this to myself until it's branded into my brain.

I hold the small stick in front of my face once again to see the results. I squint my eyes and pull it closer under the impression this will help me find an error. There is a plus sign and a minus sign. *Shit.* Pregnant. My heart leaps into my throat, the temperature in the room raises a hundred degrees. I'm going to be sick.

I groan loudly, covering my face with my hands and sit on the edge of the tub, silently freaking out. I'm going to cry.

Breathe, Kelsey, just breathe. Yep, there's no holding the tears back. What am I going to do? This can't be happening.

I can't be pregnant. I'm only twenty-two. I don't have a full-time job or insurance. I'm a bartender paying for college. I live in a small, two-bedroom apartment with my best friend because I can't afford a place on my own. I can't afford a baby. Clearly this test is a dud. I'd better take another to be sure.

"Kelsey? What's taking so long?" Sara asks from the behind the bathroom door. "I'm ready to crack this bottle of wine open and celebrate the fact we have overactive imaginations!"

Her voice startles me into motion and I stand quickly to open the second test. We went to the store solely to buy pregnancy tests, but ended up purchasing two bottles of Moscoto as well. We had high hopes this was just a really bad case of food poisoning.

"Oh, I uh …" Crap. Sara may be acting fully supportive now, but I know she will freak out as much as I am if tell her I am definitely pregnant—with her cousin's baby, no less. I never answered her questions earlier, and she won't waste time asking them again. She will drink both bottles right in front of me after I give her the answers.

I can't think fast enough for an excuse. Wiping away the tears that managed to sneak out with the back of my hand, I turn the sink on, letting the water run on full blast to hide my sniffles. "I just turned some water on, hopefully that will give my body some encouragement," I tell her, hoping she believes me.

"I told you to drink lots of water first! Did you listen to me? Noooo, you were too anxious to take the test." She pauses and neither of us says anything. She must have grown tired of waiting because she tells me to yell if I need her before I hear the sound of her bare feet against the tile floor fade as she leaves.

The fact that I can't even bring myself to tell my best friend that the first test is positive tells me that if the second one matches, I have a lot of growing up to do and I better do it fast.

How am I going to tell Ethan?

I turn the water off after I've taken care of business and set the stick on the counter as I wait for the longest three minutes of my life to pass.

Ethan

My father is riding my ass more and more lately. I avoid his calls and keep the ones we do have to a minimum, telling him only what he wants to hear, like all the other times. I can't keep lying to him because he's smart. I think he's already on to me and I need to tell someone. I need someone to tell me how to fix this mess I've made. My left leg bounces uncontrollably as I drive to the gym.

"Can I ask you something?" Logan looks at me curiously.

"Sure," I say, turning onto the gym's road.

"Why do you want to buy a house here? You always hated this place."

"Things change. People change. I have a reason to stay here now."

"Yeah, but you started the paperwork on the house before you and Kelsey hooked up. What's going on with you two? Because I'll beat your ass if you hurt her," he says in a firm voice. I like knowing that she has had someone in her life who looks out for her, but he doesn't have to do that anymore. I'm not going anywhere, but if I want him to trust me, I need to tell him everything.

"Okay. So hear me out before you say anything and try to keep your fists out of my face until I'm done," I say, pulling into the gym's parking lot and turning off my truck.

"My dad wants to take the BA from Sara and her father." Logan snaps his head at me. The look in his eye is a good warning for how I need to word the next part. "I thought I wanted to help, but not anymore." His jaw twitches. "I didn't mean for anything to happen with Kelsey, but it did, and she means more to me than what my father wants. I've been lying to him and pretending I'm helping him when I haven't been doing anything more than what Sara asked of me. She is smart when it comes to that place, and I don't believe anyone could run it better. But now my dad is on to me, and I have this bad feeling everything is about to blow up in my face."

"Is that why you started things with Kelsey? To get dirt on Sara for your father?" he asks. "Because if you're still looking, you're not going to find anything."

"No. Everything that has happened between Kelsey and me has nothing to do with my father. And I want Sara and my uncle to keep the bar. Grandpa gave it to them for reason; my father doesn't deserve it. I just … Kelsey doesn't know any of this and I don't know how to tell her."

"Well, you better tell Kelsey soon because if she finds out what you're up to from anyone else, she won't see things clearly, and she won't be as calm as I am. Now if you're done being a chicken shit and causing a whole lot of drama in my life, let's go kick some ass on the court. Oh, and grow a fucking pair. Tell your dad to go to hell." He gets out and slams the door shut.

He's right. Max Connelly can fuck off. Kelsey is more important, and it's time I started acting like it. I'll tell her everything tonight. If she feels that same about me as I do about her, she'll understand.

* * *

I pick Kelsey up for dinner and ever since she got in my truck, she's been acting weird. She hasn't spoken much, and every restaurant I mention, she's against. It started to snow first thing this morning, and the roads are getting icy. I hadn't wanted to drive far, but now we're going down the road with no specific destination in mind.

I plan to take her any place she wants tonight. I trust that she will believe me, but having her in a good mood when I tell her why I originally came to help Sara with the bar will help.

My hands are sweaty as I grip the steering wheel. I can't wait any longer. I need to just tell her. I glance over to see her eyes are glazed over as if she is about to cry.

"Are you sure everything's okay?" I ask her for the hundredth time. Last time she snapped at me, but I don't know what else to say.

She lets out a frustrated sigh that sounds exaggerated.

"Yes, I'm fine, Now will you please stop asking me that?"

"You're very snappy, and to me that means you're not fine."

"Snappy," she huffs. "That's a polite way of calling me a

bitch." She crosses her arms. Her eyes narrow as she fixes them on me, and I'm quickly regretting what I said.

"I don't mean it like that. You're just … acting standoffish. That's all."

"Let's just drop it, okay? We can just go to the BA or something. It doesn't need to be a special night," she says and her body freezes. "Wait, never mind. Go wherever you want."

If she wants to go the BA, I'll take her to the BA. I don't like it when she isn't happy, and I will do anything to change that.

She doesn't say anything as we find a parking spot. Nor does she say anything when we join Logan at one of the tables inside. She just sits in silence, staring off into space, and I really wish I knew what she is thinking right now. I reach my hand under the table to give her thigh a light squeeze. If I knew what was wrong, maybe I could fix it.

Whatever mood she's in, it isn't giving me the encouragement I need to tell her about my dad. I don't want to make her even more upset, and right now that seems to be all I'm doing. Tonight is definitely not the night I tell her, but fuck, I'd better do it before it's too late.

CHAPTER TWENTY-THREE

Kelsey

"Ethan."

The deep boom of a man's voice causes us all to jump. Standing next to our table is a man whose presence instantly makes my skin crawl. He stands tall, with dark hair and even darker eyes. He scans the table, pausing briefly on each one of us with those disapproving eyes. When his eyes reach Ethan, they immediately turn to disgust.

Who is this man?

"So, this is what you've been up to." He stretches his arms to his sides and twists slightly. "And here I thought my son was successfully running a business."

Son.

Ethan sits still with his head hanging in front of him. He slowly withdraws his hand from mine, and his father watches him the entire time. Now is probably not the best time to make my announcement. *Oh hey, you're Ethan's father, nice to meet you. Guess what? Ethan's going to be a father. Congrats, Grandpa.*

"Ahhh, and this, I assume, is the reason you haven't been returning my calls," his father says, raising an eyebrow directly at me.

I swallow hard and take a breath. Ethan hasn't moved. An awkward silence falls over the table, and Logan slides out of his chair without saying a word. What could Ethan's father be so upset about? Ethan's only covering until Sara comes back—it's not like he's preparing to take over. And if my father spoke to me that way, I wouldn't return his calls either.

"Don't be a coward, Ethan. Look me in the eye when I'm speaking to you."

Ethan slowly lifts his head. His eyes briefly meet mine before he looks directly at his father.

"Better. Now get off that stool and follow me to the office," he demands.

Ethan doesn't say a word. He just nods and obeys.

I don't move from my seat until the office door is closed completely. The way Ethan is acting is completely strange. Why would he be afraid of his father? I spring off my stool and quickly make my way to the back room to find Logan. Something is going on and I am going to find out what it is.

"Logan, where are you?"

"Geez, I'm right here, Kels, so stop yelling," he says, stepping out from behind the linen rack. I position my body right in front of him, putting my hand on my hips with my elbows out. I block any chance he has of getting by.

"What's going on? What's Mr. Connelly doing here?" I shout. "And don't tell me you don't know, because you slipped away from the table so fast, I know you know what's going on."

Logan shakes his head and tries to take a step around me, but I shove my hip into his. "Tell me what's going on, please, Logan. I've never seen Ethan act that way around anyone, and I'm worried." My voice is beginning to sound desperate, and when a tear sneaks its way out, Logan releases a breath.

"It's not my place to say anything, Kelsey. Ethan will tell you when the time is right, and with his dad here, I'm guessing that time is pretty close. Just wait till his dad leaves, okay?"

Logan squeezes past me. *Wait till his father leaves.* What does that mean? His father just got here.

Ethan wouldn't even look at me. It was like I didn't exist.

I storm out of the storage room, marching right past Logan, heading straight for the office. Someone's going to give me answers, and they're going to do it right this minute. My patience has completely disappeared. I intentionally ignore Logan as he begs me to wait with him. What part of "I don't want to wait" doesn't he understand?

I raise my fist to knock on the door and stop midair as the yelling on the other side startles me.

"What in the hell were you thinking?" Ethan's father's voice gets louder. "Getting involved with an employee. Your actions are disappointing. I thought you were better than this."

Deciding it might be best to wait a minute, I do the next best thing. I eavesdrop. I lean my ear as close as I can to hear the end of their conversation.

"She's not just some employee, Dad, so stop referring to her that way!"

"I hope you mean as much to her as she does to you. Tell

me, what did she say when you told her why you're here? Did she understand and support you?"

The silence that follows is terrifying. *You're here to help your cousin, Ethan! Tell him.*

"I figured. I didn't think she would support your intentions to pull this bar out from under her best friend."

What did he say?

"Dad, stop!"

"No, you stop! You're going to follow through on this plan and you're going to do it without any distractions, do you hear me? You're going to find me the evidence I need to steal this bar from my brother even if it means using that little brunette out there to do it."

My entire body starts to shake as I take a step back. *Ethan's been using me.*

I stumble when I bump into a nearby table, and my unbalanced body falls over the surface and onto the ground. I see Logan in front of me and his lips are moving, but I don't hear anything.

All this time, I thought this was forever. I know it hasn't been that long, but I believed Ethan when he said this was real. We were going to be a happy family. Turns out I thought wrong, and he doesn't really want me. He is just using me to make his father proud, and now I'm left alone and pregnant.

When the office door opens and I see Ethan rushing toward me, I push myself off the ground and dash for the door. It's still snowing out so I should grab my coat, but I'm in such a hurry I don't care. I run straight for my apartment across the street.

"Kelsey, stop!" Ethan yells behind me, but I don't listen. "Stop!"

There's so much I want to say right now. I should just lay it out there and get the whole situation over with. I start to turn mid-step, but my foot catches a patch of ice, and everything goes black.

Ethan

I keep pacing back and forth in the waiting room at the hospital. Watching Kelsey slip wrecked me. I rushed to try to catch her, but I didn't make it. Her head bounced off the icy pavement, and I didn't question what to do. I laid her in the backseat of my truck and brought her straight to the emergency room. Had I been thinking clearly, I would have left her and called someone. If she has a concussion, I might have made things worse.

I need to call Sara. I need to call a lot of people. It's time I confess what's going on. Even if Kelsey didn't remember what happened, I won't lie to her. I will tell her everything. I will tell her the truth. But what if she doesn't remember anything ... or anyone? I run my hand through my hair and begin to pace some more.

I'm alone in the waiting room, which is a good thing. I could go off at any moment and having someone around to witness it or become my punching bag isn't a good idea. When I hear the door to the waiting room open, my fists are in balls before I'm fully turned around to face the newcomer.

Logan takes a step inside, closing the door quietly behind him. He takes a breath.

"The nurse out there says she's going to be fine. She woke up, but they say she needs to rest. They want to keep her overnight just to be safe. All in all it's just a rough bump on the head and nothing to worry about."

I nod and take a seat. Not worry about her? I can't do that. She's always on my mind. Knowing she's lying in that room because of me and I can't do a thing to help her, it tears me apart.

"I called Sara," Logan adds as he sits in the chair next to mine. "She was already back in town so she will be here soon." He lets out a deep breath. "You're going to have to tell her everything you know. Sara won't accept that this was some freak accident. I think there is a reason Sara is already back, something to do with Kelsey."

"What do you mean? What's wrong with Kelsey?' I ask, rising from my seat.

"Calm down, okay?" Logan says as he also stands. He puts a hand on my shoulder, but I shrug it off and step away from him.

"Look, man. You both have secrets. Hers are just a little more recent than yours. But you both need to grow the hell up and start being honest with each other. Your relationship won't make it if you keep things from each other."

I know what he's saying is right. I knew it before he had to say it. I just never did anything about it.

"That's if we still have a relationship. You didn't see her face when I walked out of that office. She heard everything and … well, I don't think she's going to forgive me for this."

"She also thinks you were using her. We both know that isn't true," Logan points out.

"I never used her. Everything we had was real," I say through clenched teeth. *Shit.* Logan's only agreeing with me and I'm being a dick. I sit and lean my head back against the wall, closing my eyes. I don't know how to control the way I feel right now. My whole life is lying in a hospital bed. Without her, I'm nothing.

We sit in silence; no one comes into the waiting room and neither of us leaves. Logan's cellphone chirps and minutes later Sara's bursting through the door.

"You," she growls, pointing at me. "What did you do?"

I stand quickly as Sara marches up to me. She's less than half my size, but when she's mad, she can be a real terror.

"Before you try to beat him up, you should hear him out," Logan tells her as he steps in front of me. "And I mean hear him all the way through. No cutting him off mid-sentence."

Sara pins him with an intense glare but reluctantly takes a seat next to Logan. I sit down on his other side and tell her everything. Including the part where I fell in love with Kelsey Brian.

CHAPTER TWENTY-FOUR

Kelsey

I wake up to the sound of a machine beeping next to my head. I'm glad the noise is soft because I have a killer headache. My eyes flutter as I attempt to open them. Large windows to the right of my bed fill the room with sunlight, and it takes a moment for my eyes to adjust. There's a round table in the far corner under the window that has flowers filling the entire surface. Sara is sitting in the blue chair next to the table, her arms wrapped around her legs as she hugs them close to her chest, her head buried behind them.

The bed squeaks as I try to push myself into a seated position. I give up quickly and grab the remote next to my bed. I always wanted to use one of these. I just didn't want to be admitted to a hospital to do it. Sara lifts her head and squints at the light until she sees me and moves to stand next to my bed."You're awake." She smiles at me. "The doctors thought you would wake up again last night, but you just kept sleeping. I was getting worried."

"Did you stay here all night?"

"Yeah, Logan called me." She looks down at her watch. "It's a little after seven now. I should probably go let someone know you're awake and call your parents," she says and leaves the room.

How long have I been in here? I remembering falling, but I don't remember coming here. Sara returns followed by a nurse who looks like she isn't much older than we are, her bleached blonde hair pulled into a bun and wearing pale blue scrubs.

"Hi there," she says. "How are you feeling?"

"Tired, but I feel good."

"That's good news. You suffered a mild concussion when you bumped your head, but things are looking better. It looks like you were quite exhausted. We've just been waiting for you to wake up so we can run a few tests and send you home. I'll let the doctor know you're awake. Can I get you anything in the meantime?"

I shake my head to let her know I'm fine. When really I'm not fine because I know the conversation Sara wants to have, and I'm not ready to have it. I thought I knew what I was going to do about the baby, but now—after what I heard—I don't know much of anything anymore. The nurse closes the door behind her and, with one leg bent on the bed and the other hanging to the floor, Sara takes a seat to face me.

"I know things probably seem really unbalanced right now, but I think you should still tell Ethan what's going on."

"I don't want to talk to Ethan." Yes, I'm mad at him. I'm angrier than I've ever been in my whole life. I want to scream at him, hurt him the way he hurt me. I don't want to share the news that not twenty-four hours ago made me the happiest and most scared person on earth. He doesn't deserve to be happy too. He used me.

Sara releases a heavy sigh. "Look, Kels, I'm mad at him too, alright? He's been up to some super-shady behavior, and I'm not going to forgive him easily for it, but he has the right to know."

I don't have time to argue with her before the nurse returns. She has a clipboard in her hand and she's writing something down.

"Okay, Kelsey, I just need to ask you a few more questions before we run those tests." A knock on the room's door stops her mid-sentence, and we all turn to see who it is.

Ethan's standing in the doorway, wearing the same clothes he had on yesterday, and his hair is a mess. His eyes are glazed and red, and his face has a slight stubble. His entire appearance looks exhausted. *Good.* He looks how I feel.

"Excuse me, sir, visiting hours haven't started yet. Only family is allowed right now," the nurse says sweetly to him.

"I'm her cousin," he says, pointing in my direction. Sara's sitting next to me and since he wasn't specific, the nurse assumes he is talking about me. She nods and he steps into the room, moving cautiously around the bed to stand on my other side. I don't have the energy to argue with anyone right now. He can stay, but I'm not talking to him.

"Alright, Ms. Brian, is there any medication you're taking or any medical concerns we need to know about before we start?" the nurse asks.

Damn it. I should have asked him to leave.

I drop my chin to my chest and take a deep breath. I have to say it. I have to tell her the truth. Any one of those tests could harm me or the baby.

"I'm pregnant," I blurt out and the room fills with silence. My eyes instantly search for Ethan's and I watch as his face crumbles.

That's the only look I need to see to be reminded that this entire thing between us has been a sham. A tear slips by, but I control the full waterworks because the one piece keeping me strong now is this baby.

Ethan

Pregnant.

I swallow hard as I lean against the wall next to Kelsey's bed. Kelsey's pregnant. *With my baby.* I take a couple of concentrated breaths before I look at her. Her gaze is pointing down to her hands laced in her lap. I see the tears running down her cheeks, and her chest moving slowly with each breath she takes. My heart breaks as the nurse looks between Kelsey and me before she quietly excuses herself from the room.

"Why didn't you tell me?" I step toward her.

Kelsey swallows but doesn't look up.

"Ethan, you should probably leave for a bit. Give everyone some time to process this." Sara is standing in front of me, speaking quietly. I force myself to look at her. Leave? She can't be serious. Kelsey and I have a lot to talk about. How can she not see this? I just found out I'm going to be a father, and she wants me to leave.

"I'm not going anywhere," I say firmly and take a step around her toward Kelsey. Sara grabs my arm, and I snap my head to look her in the eye. What doesn't she understand?

"Ethan, please," she pleads. I stare at her for a moment

then look back to Kelsey. She's watching us as the tears continue to spill from her eyes.

"Is this what you want, for me to leave?" I ask her. She keeps her red, swollen eyes locked on mine for what feels like the longest moment of my life and then nods.

I want to yell. I want to hit something or even slam her door as I go, but I don't. I don't say anything as I leave her room. My heart feels like she just gripped it and squeezed as hard she could.

I haven't cried in a long time. I'm a man and we don't cry. I step into the elevator and the doors close in front of me. The car is filled with silence, giving my mind more power to yell and scream at me for everything I have done wrong. I want to cry. Cry for the way my heart feels. I want to cry because Kelsey's in pain because of me. She's pregnant because of me. She looks terrified because of me. And now she doesn't want anything to do with me, and I want to cry because I just lost the best thing that ever happened to me and I don't know how to fix it.

The one thing I do know I need to do is get my father out of my life. When I get home to find him parked in my driveway, the anger building inside of me urges me to punch his teeth out.

He opens his door, standing to glare at me. "I sent you here for one thing. Look at the mess you made."

"You need to leave."

"I'm not going anywhere until I get—"

"Get the fuck off my driveway and out of my life!" I yell. His head jerks back as he stares at me.

"Excuse me? I've done nothing but give your spoiled,

ungrateful ass everything you have today. You have no right to speak to me that way."

"I don't want anything from you, except for you to leave. Take it all. The truck, the house, the bike. I don't care. The one person who means anything to me is lying in a hospital bed with my unborn child, and she wouldn't be there if I hadn't wanted to be accepted as your son so goddamn bad. None of that matters to me now. You don't matter to me. Just leave."

"Oh that's brilliant, Ethan. Add to your mess by knocking up the—"

I step toward him, fists clenched at my sides. "Leave! Get the fuck out of here. If I have to say it again, I will hit you and won't stop until someone drags you away from me."

His eyes glance at my hands before he points at me.

"You are not welcome in my home, ever again."

I throw my hands up as he gets in his car and backs away.

I will gladly never see that man again. If I have any chance of redeeming myself with Kelsey in order for us to have a real family, my father needs to be as far away from me as I can get him.

CHAPTER TWENTY-FIVE

Kelsey

The next few weeks go slowly. I decline Sara's mother's invitation to join them for Thanksgiving. I don't want to chance seeing Ethan. My parents came home early from their trip, and my mother is more excited about my news than my father. He's being a total Scrooge this holiday season, but I don't care. I never expect him to be happy.

There's no way I'm staying at their house anymore. I don't want to be anywhere near Ethan. Thinking about him is hard enough. I would lose it if I saw him. But I miss him. I'm so angry and confused; I don't understand how I can miss him. He's the reason we're in this spot to begin with. My cell-phone rings on the stand next to my bed. I glance over to see Ethan's name flashing across the screen. *Again.* I don't reach for my phone but instead I sink down into my bed and cover myself completely with the sheets.

The finalist dinner came and went, and although they offered me the position and I accepted it, I can't even force myself to be happy about it. It's the one thing in my life that's actually working out. For as much as I had looked forward to that night, my mind is still in such a fog over everything that's happened, it almost doesn't feel real.

"Kelsey?" Sara pokes her head inside my bedroom door. "I'm going to make spaghetti for dinner. Do you want some?"

My stomach rumbles at the word *spaghetti*. Sounds like my little one is going to be a lover of Italian food just like her mother. I'm almost positive it's a girl.

"I'm going to take that as a yes." Sara gives a slight laugh from the door and then leaves.

Once the door closes, I pull the sheets off my face. The red light at the top of my phone screen is blinking. I have a voicemail.

I stare at my phone, trying to decide what to do. Ethan leaves a voicemail every time he calls. I never listen to them and when my mailbox is full, I delete them unheard.

I crawl out of bed and stand in front of the full-length mirror behind my bedroom door. When I was at the hospital I found out I was eight weeks along, which makes me almost eleven weeks now. That means I got pregnant the night of the pool table and my due date is early June. It also means I'm an idiot because I didn't know for eight weeks. I should have figured it out sooner. I turn to my side and lift up my shirt. I don't look any different, but I feel like a whole new person.

I have my first real doctor's appointment next week, and Sara is going with me. Every day she tells me I'm making a mistake by not including Ethan, but I try my best to ignore her. She's still mad at him, but I think she's even more annoyed that I don't want him there. I don't want him around me or the baby at all. He was pretending the whole time we were together and never wanted me to begin with. I don't want the burden of him pretending he wants a family too.

I just wish I could pretend that I hadn't fallen in love with him and that my heart doesn't hurt when I think of him. Most of all, I wish I didn't miss him.

Ethan

It's crazy how disappointed a person can be with himself. We are responsible for making our own choices. Even when we know the outcome can be bad, most of the time, we still make mistakes.

I knew what could happen the longer I kept things from Kelsey, and for some reason, I still never found a time to tell her. Now, here I am, lying on the couch in my living room in the dark and feeling angry with myself because I made a mistake. A big mistake.

It's been almost two months since Logan told me about her first doctor's appointment. The one where she first heard the baby's heartbeat and the one I should have gone to with her. But she still won't answer my calls. I've missed Thanksgiving, Christmas, and New Year's. We were supposed to spend them all together. Now, I may never get the chance.

I've considered countless times going over to her apartment and demand she talk to me. I should do it, because after everything, keeping a child from their father is bullshit, but Sara keeps reassuring me Kelsey will come around and I need to give her space. Two months feels like plenty of time to get your space. I need to just face it: Kelsey wants nothing to do with me. Not even as the father of our baby.

Sara's been kind enough to keep me employed at the BA,

but she gave Kelsey a new position keeping the books and lets her do it from their apartment. The fall semester ended, meaning Kelsey's finally done with college and will walk in the spring ceremony to get her degree. She got the columnist job. I wanted to call to congratulate her—for moments like that, I should be there with her, but I never dialed her number

I'm also lucky that Logan has been sharing bits and pieces of what Kelsey has been up to and how she's feeling. He threatens me each time that Sara can never find out what he is doing. More secrets. That's what got me into this whole mess.

A knock at my door doesn't pull me off the couch. I don't care who's here. If it's not Kelsey, they don't matter. The knock quickly turns into pounding until whoever it is gives up and just lets themselves inside.

"Dude, really, get off the couch," Logan says as he walks closer and then stops to bury his face in his elbow and wave his free hand in front of him. "If that's you who smells like garbage, we have problems. Come on, get up."

"I'm good," I tell him.

"No, you're not. Look at you, sitting all pathetic on the couch. Not giving a damn. Haven't showered, haven't shaved, and haven't—"

"I don't have a reason to do any of those things. Drop it," I say, rising quickly to get in his face.

"Well … at least I got you off the couch." He pushes me away from him. "Now go shower."

"No," I argue, letting my body drop back onto the sofa.

"Alright," Logan steps toward me and yanks on my arm. Like a little kid, I pull back, lift my foot to his stomach, and push him away before I jump to my feet.

"Dude, what the—"

Logan grabs my arms and pulls me in front of him then shoves me from the back.

"Get in the shower now, Ethan. Kelsey and Sara are going to get some food and we're going to be at the café when they get there."

Now he has my full attention.

"She doesn't want anything to do with me, Logan. It will only make things worse."

He doesn't respond right away and his silence lets me know he isn't giving up.

"Is that what you want?" he asks.

"What?"

"To give up. To just let her go. To let her live her life without you."

"That's not what I want. That's what *she* wants."

Logan shakes his head. "So, you *are* giving up. I have to tell you, I think it's weak and stupid and you're an idiot. Stop acting like a girl and being all dramatic. Go get what you want. Don't take no for an answer."

"I'm not being a girl," I tell him and walk straight up the stairs to take a shower.

* * *

We pull into a parking space next to the diner downtown. Logan turns off his truck.

"Let's go."

"What if she causes a scene?" I ask.

"She won't. The only person causing a scene right now is you being afraid to go in there."

I get out of the truck and walk past him into the coffee

shop. I'm over all this "you're acting like a bitch" talk.

The smell of coffee beans is overwhelming when I walk inside. It takes me less than five seconds to find Sara. My heart drops in my chest when I notice she's sitting alone. She smiles at me and waves me over. I walk slowly, disappointed because Kelsey isn't here.

"Hurry, sit," Sara demands. May as well do what everyone else tells me since my own choices haven't ended well. "She can't run if you're already sitting."

Run.

What is she talking about?

"I have her purse, too, so she has to come to the table—oh shh, shh here she comes." Sara waves her hands in my face. Kelsey stands just a few tables away. She looks perfect, wearing blue jeans and a plain white t-shirt snug against her belly.

She stops when she sees me, and for a minute I think I see her eyes tearing up. Probably a pregnancy thing. I've read a little about it, but I'm still hoping they are tears of joy at seeing me. Her face has no expression as she walks to our table.

"Hi," I say when she stops next to Sara's chair. She squats down, grabs her purse, then walks away.

"Kelsey, wait!" I shout as I follow her out of the coffee shop. "Please talk to me. I messed up, I know I did, but—"

"But nothing, Ethan. I don't want this baby to grow up in a lie or to suffer like I have."

"It wasn't a lie. Nothing with you was a lie. I love you." I grab her hand and pull her close. "I love you more than anything, and I will spend the rest of my life making it up to you. Please. Please give me that chance."

Tears flow over her cheeks as she looks away and time stands still. She takes a moment to catch her breath.

"I'm not going to keep you from your baby, Ethan. No matter what happens, this baby deserves a father. You will always be a part of my life, but I can't trust you, Ethan, and I … I don't want this. I don't want us."

"Just give me five minutes to explain. I never intended to hurt you. I just wanted my dad's approval."

"You had more than enough chances before this all happened to talk to me. To trust me. But you didn't and this is what happened. I'm sorry, Ethan."

And just like that, I watch her walk away without fighting. She's given me more chances than I can ask for, and the only thing left for me to do is wait until she decides to change her mind. Deep down, I am scared that she won't.

CHAPTER TWENTY-SIX

Kelsey

I have another doctor's appointment today, and I'm still a blubbering mess over running into Ethan. Seeing him at the café pulled every emotion I've worked hard to bury out into the open. I grab a Kleenex and gently try to fix my makeup, but the tears keep coming and ruin it. After giving up, I wander down the hall to the kitchen and find Sara sitting at the table in her pajamas with her computer in front of her. She looks up and frowns.

"Hey, how many times do I need to remind you that stress isn't good for you or the baby?" she says softly as she gets up to give me a hug.

"It's not like I'm trying to be stressed. I blame you this time for the whole lunch fiasco yesterday." This causes her to smile, and she sits back down, tucking one leg under the other.

"I just want you to be happy. And I thought you were

happy with Ethan. I just wanted to help get things back on track. Don't you think you've punished him enough?"

"Just because you've already forgiven him doesn't mean I can, too."

My eyes start to tear up again when I see her sad smile, but I quickly pull myself together at a knock at the door. I open the door slowly and the waterworks come back when I find my brother Conner, standing in the hallway.

He's taller than I remember, but his hair is still the same brown as mine, only curly and a tad bit shaggy, and his dark brown eyes feel like home. He pulls me into a hug as I sob into his white shirt.

"Calm down. It's okay," he says and then holds me at shoulder length to look me in the eye. "Aren't these supposed to be the happiest moments in your life?" he asks and I laugh.

"You try being pregnant. Nothing happy about your clothes not fitting, throwing up at almost every smell, and—"

"Doing it alone is your choice, Kelsey," Sara adds from her spot at the table. "Hey, Conner. It's good to see you," she says, then shuts her laptop and leaves us alone in the kitchen.

I close the door, point to the sofa, and grab a couple of waters before I join him.

"Alone, huh? What happened to the dad?" Conner asks.

"He … wasn't who I thought he was," I say, lowering my head. Conner never knew Ethan that well, but he knew him well enough to know who I'm talking about.

"Did you know I have a son?" he asks and I look at him with surprise. Conner is never the kind of person to beat around the bush. "Yep, you're an aunt. For almost two years now."

How did I not know any of this? My little brother has a kid and no one tells me!

"I just found out about him two weeks ago. His name is Jake," he adds and gives me a weak smile as he pulls out a photo. The little boy in the phone looks just like him as he sits on the swing with a big smile and dirt all over his face.

"I went to tell Mom and Dad first, but Mom wouldn't stop rambling on about what's going on with you. I came here as soon as she stopped talking." He laughs for a split second before his face falls serious again. "I'm not going to give you some big lecture, but I missed out on two years of his life and those are years I'll never get back. We both know I'm not perfect and I probably did something to screw up bad enough she didn't want me around. It sucks. I would do anything for this kid, and I wish his mother would have told me so that no matter what our past was, we could have given the family thing a try." He takes a deep breath. "But it sucks most of all that this little boy was caught in the middle of it and spent two years without a father. Don't take your anger with this baby's father out on your child. He or she didn't do anything to deserve it, but they deserve to be happy, just like you. They deserve a family."

I never thought I'd be so excited for a doctor's appointment. Today I find out if my baby is a boy or girl. My fingers are crossed as I wait not so patiently, hoping he or she is in a position to know for sure. I want to call Ethan to tell him about it and invite him to join me, but I'm scared.

My mind is still going haywire since my brother left. I'm

excited for him and his new son. And I hope things work out for him. What he said to me, about not being in his son's life made sense, but I just don't know if I have in me to risk being hurt again.

"It's a girl," the doctor's voice distracts me as he runs the scanner over my belly and watches the screen. "See right there, she's bending over for us. No mistaking this one. You're definitely having a girl."

Tears form in my eyes. My baby is now my little girl, and there isn't anyone here to enjoy this moment with.

That's your own fault, Kelsey.

"We'll get you a copy so you can share it with your friends and family," he says, leaving the room. I adjust my shirt over my round belly that's now extremely noticeable to everyone. I was never hiding it, but there was a time where you couldn't tell whether I was pregnant or putting on some extra weight.

I walk down the short hallway back to the waiting room to make my next appointment. There's a man and a woman sitting together, both bent over with their attention on the baby carrier in front of them. The woman laughs and the man kisses her temple. I'll never have that. I'll never get to experience what it's like to be a happy family. I sit down as I wait my turn, but I can't take my eyes away from this new family.

Ethan hasn't given up on us. God, he told me he loved me. I know he didn't say it just because I'm pregnant. The emotion that came with it went straight to my heart. I was mad then, but right now, I'm thinking clearer.

I shouldn't have just walked away. I should have given him a chance to explain himself. Just because we can't get a relationship right the first time, or second, or even third doesn't mean we can't make one work in the end.

"Ms. Brian," the nurse behind the counter calls my name. The new mother gives me a small, sad smile. She must have noticed me watching her and how alone I am.

I give my paper to the nurse, she types a few buttons, and we schedule my next appointment. Another nurse hands me the picture of my baby girl. At the door, I take a final look back at the family. I could have that. I could be happy. It's clear what I need to do.

I close myself inside my car and pull out my phone. I need to call Sara and find out where Ethan is. I've been wrong this whole time and hope it's not too late for him to take me back.

"Hi, how was it?" Sara answers.

"Do you know where Ethan is?" I ask her instead of answering her question.

"What?"

"Ethan, Sara … where is he?"

I hear her whispering—to whom I don't know, but I have a pretty good guess. She giggles and tells whoever she's with to stop what they're doing.

"He's at home," she says into the phone with a laugh. "Why do you ask?"

"I need to talk to him. I need to fix everything," I say and hang up, tossing the phone onto the passenger seat as I drive straight for Ethan's house.

I stand outside his door waiting as patiently as I can. He has to be home. He has to answer this door right now. I've made countless mistakes in my life, but having a life without Ethan isn't even an option anymore. I want it all. And I want it all with him. *Please. Please answer the door.*

. . .

Ethan

I really hope Logan isn't messing with me. On cue, Kelsey's car pulls into my driveway. I don't take my eyes off her as she runs to the door, bundled in a winter coat and pair of jeans. Logan warned me, but Kelsey coming here doesn't really sink in until I see her.

I stand with my hand over the knob, giving myself a quick pep talk before I open the door. I'm finally coming to terms with the way she wants things. She and I won't be together and our baby will grow up in separate homes. I remind myself how hard it's going to be when I see her, when I look into her eyes, and she doesn't want me back. She doesn't want us. And I need to stop convincing myself she'll change her mind.

I turn the knob slowly and open the door. Kelsey looks just as beautiful as any other day I see her. Only this time, her coat is hanging loose at her sides and her belly is poking out toward me.

I swallow hard. Forget what I just said. I'm not giving up.

"Did you mean it?" she asks, not missing a beat.

"Mean what?" I gesture for her to come inside.

"That you loved me."

I take her hand before she can walk inside any farther, turning her to face me until her eyes line up with mine.

"Yes."

"Then how could you hurt me like that?" A tear slips down her check and I brush it away with my thumb.

"I've asked myself that question every day since we've been apart, and I can't come up with any other explanation other than I spent so much time willing you to trust me that I failed to trust myself or to trust that you would understand. I feared your reaction. Losing you terrified me, and in the end, no matter what choice I made, I was wrong."

More tears drip off her cheek as she sniffles.

"But you trust me now?"

I nod.

"I was wrong, too, about everything," she says as she steps forward and reaches for my hand. "I love you and I want this. I want us."

"I want us, too," I say, kissing her forehead and wrapping my arms around her. "Promise me that next time something bad happens—even though I hope it never does, but just in case—promise me we'll talk, we'll tell each other everything. No secrets and no lies. It's us, all in or nothing."

"I promise," she says without hesitation before kissing me. I pull her close and feel a flutter against my stomach. She giggles, breaking the kiss, and looks down to her stomach.

"She must be as excited as I am right now."

She.

She grabs my hand, pushing my fingers against the side of her belly. The flutter happens again, and I swallow back the tear working its way out. Kelsey swings her purse around and pulls out a small photo to show me.

"Is this our—?"

"Daughter, yes, it is," she finishes.

Her eyes are bright and watering as they look into mine. Everything that's happened leading to this moment doesn't matter anymore. Everything I want is standing right in front of me. This time, it's going to be forever.

EPILOGUE

Six Months Later…

Kelsey

I sit in one of chairs at the patio table in Sara's parents' backyard. It's her twenty-third birthday, and her parents invited everyone they know to her party, everyone except Ethan's father. No one has made amends with him, not even Ethan. I don't think anyone cares. The only thing Ethan is still trying to mend is his relationship with his brothers. They've promised to visit soon, but I'm okay with waiting a few years.

Laugher surrounds me and I take it all in. I have a feeling they're celebrating something besides Sara's birthday and are going to announce something big since they also invited their own friends, but it's yet to happen. My money is on the new bar her father bought in Colorado. I'm not supposed to know about it, but I bet anything that's his gift to her.

Sara is patiently getting her picture taken over and over,

giving her best smile each time. "You'd think she is some kind of celebrity." Ethan chuckles next to me as Clara coos in my arms. I smile as he leans over to kiss my cheek. It still amazes me how lucky I am to have someone like him in my life.

We eloped the week before Clara was born because I wanted to have the same last name as all my children, but we still plan on having a big wedding. Ethan's just as excited as I am for the future. I couldn't ask for a better husband or father for our daughter.

"She wasn't gone that long. It's not like she's some world traveler now. Mrs. Mulligan has been following her all afternoon asking questions. Doesn't she know other people missed her, too?" Logan says, taking another pull off his beer.

After Ethan and I got back together, Sara left for another trip, and Logan has been the most upset over it. I give Ethan a quick glance and try to hide my smile before he sits foreword, resting his elbows on his knees.

"She's been back for weeks. Three actually, since she came back the day Clara was born." Logan points to the small blessing in my arms then glances back to Sara.

"She probably hasn't seen Mrs. Mulligan, or Mrs. Mulligan assumes she's already shared these stories with everyone else," I say.

Logan lets out a frustrated growl and gets up. "Or Mrs. Mulligan is still just a nosey neighbor. I'm getting another beer—do you want one?" he asks, looking at Ethan.

"No thanks. As long as Kelsey isn't drinking, I'm not drinking," he says, reaching his arms around me and Clara, kissing my shoulder.

Logan watches us a moment. He takes a breath, swallows, and nods his head. He gives us a half-smile that quickly fades at the sound of Sara's laughter, and he storms into the house. *That man has got it bad.*

My mother takes Clara from me, covering her in grandma kisses. Surprisingly, both she and my father have made the effort to see Clara every day. It helps that I now live across the street from them. My father has also been acting more fatherly to me in the last few months that he ever has. Mom's convinced it's because he finally accepts that I'm a grown woman now. She's probably right. I've let it go because I don't want Clara to grow up without her grandfather just because of our past.

I take this opportunity of my mother watching Clara to get some alone time with Ethan. I lace my fingers with his as I pull him toward the side of the house. We don't need to hide our affection anymore, but being sneaky is much more fun.

We quickly make our way around the house, Ethan unwinds his hands from mine, moving them to my waist as he walks behind me. I can feel the warmth of his breath as he's about to say something into my ear, only he doesn't. We're too distracted by the laughter we hear coming from the trees. Ethan pulls me close to the corner of the house as we check to see who it is.

Logan steps around a tree with a wide grin and scans the area before he reaches his arm behind him. *I thought he went inside.* Small fingers latch onto his and Sara steps into view. She looks at Logan, happier than I have ever seen her, and she kisses him.

I open my mouth to confront them, but nothing comes out because Ethan quickly covers my lips with his and pulls me against his body. We hold on tightly to each other as we kiss passionately on the side of the house—in the same exact spot where our story started.

Life will never turn out the way we plan for it. You never expect that a moment you once thought ruined everything is only the beginning or that the worst moments are actually the best. I've shared both the good and bad with Ethan, and never once did I think I would stand in this spot with him again.

But it's true: Our happily ever after story started with just one kiss.

***

Want exclusive content delivered right to your inbox?
Subscribe to Jami's mailing list for all the book news!

Ready for Sara and Logan's story?
Start reading Just One Night today!

JUST ONE NIGHT

CHAPTER ONE

Last summer …

Sara

I'm fully aware of my own vulnerabilities. I know what I need to do to avoid them and yet, I'm about to be alone in The Black Alcove bar, BA for short, that I manage for my father, with my number one weakness. Logan Parker.

The lock clicks under Logan's fingers after the last two customers are finally out the door. Friday night of finals week is always the busiest night. What better way to celebrate passing finals and the start to summer than with a drink, right?

"I honestly thought those last two guys were never going to leave," Logan says, sauntering behind the bar. He flicks the last of the lights on, and we both squint at the brightness.

"They had so many drinks, I was beginning to think they were going to pass out here," I respond.

It's nearing two thirty in the morning, and I can't speak for Logan, but I'm exhausted and can't wait to crawl into my bed and fall asleep. This was my final semester, too. I'm officially a college graduate—minus knowing my official grades and the fact I'm choosing not to walk with the rest of the class—and although I should be joining other students my age, I'm working.

Work before play is the Connelly way.

My father taught me this motto while he and my mother were splitting up when I was ten. He told me I need to follow it so I don't make the same mistakes he did. Twelve years later, this motto follows me everywhere. The part where my mother left and never came back proves his reasoning accurate. I get the yearly birthday card from her, but that's all and I'm okay with it.

"Did you see the shirt he was wearing?" Logan asks, chuckling as he drains the sinks and begins to scrub them clean.

"Yes! Oh god. It looked exactly like that blue button up you wore every day of junior year."

"I didn't wear it every day."

"Only the ones where you were in class." I laugh, pulling up a seat as he hands me the cash drawer and turns the credit card machine toward me. I punch a few numbers and the receipt of tonight's numbers starts to print.

"Hey, that was a classy shirt. It made me look good, and if I remember right, I was wearing that shirt the day I asked you out."

"Yep, that's right, and you wore it every day that we dated, too."

"I wore different shirts that year."

"Not that I remember."

Logan quickly sprays me with the sink's hose and I squeal when the cold water splashes against my skin.

"Okay, okay, whatever happened to that shirt anyway?" I ask when he tosses me a towel, flashing the grin that tugs every emotion I've ever felt for him. And it's a lot. Especially when I know exactly where said shirt is—in my closet. I was supposed to give it back to him but never got around to it and now … well, it'd be creepy if I told him I still had it.

"It was ripped and a few of the buttons were torn off—"

"What? You loved that shirt. How did you ruin it?" I ask. I've always been curious to what happened.

"Mark Matheson actually ripped it. The night we broke up, I went to a party out at Wind River field after I left your house and started a fight. It came off somehow during the brawl and I never saw it again."

Those same emotions—joy from what we had, fear of losing him again, and hope that we could one day go back to that—flood back into my chest as I gaze up at him from my seat. His eyes flash to mine briefly before he looks away.

"What do you think would have happened if we hadn't broken up?" he asks. There's a hesitation to his voice, but when his eyes settle on me again, I see fear. He's nervous about my answer.

"Logan, I—"

I can't even finish the sentence because although I've thought of this moment time after time since high school, my heart couldn't take it again. I'll never forget the day Logan told me he couldn't have a girlfriend because his life was just beginning. He would be going away for college and didn't want to continue something he couldn't hold a promise to. That he wouldn't even try broke my heart the way any seventeen-year-old's heart would break. I thought my life was over.

It took almost our entire senior year of high school for us

to go back to the friends we were before dating. I've imagined us starting a relationship again, but I can't lose him the way I did before. Not with the friendship we have now.

"Wait, don't answer that. I just … I want you to know that breaking up with you was one of the biggest mistakes I could have made, and I'd do anything to take it back."

I blink, watching as his eyes bore into my own, and my breathing gets faster. His gaze never breaks its hold as he quickly rounds the bar.

"I'm not asking you to make a decision right now, or even tomorrow or the next day. But I am asking you to think about it."

"Logan, it's been five years. Where is this coming from?"

"Sara, come on, that spark between us—it's always been there. You're the first person I go to with good news, and I know I'm that person for you, too. We flirt more than your average friends should and that's because we've never been just friends. Never. I'm finally speaking up about it."

"Logan—" The words to disagree catch in my throat because he's right.

"Just one night, Sara. That's all I'm asking. Nothing has to happen that you don't want to, but just spend one night with me."

The fact he isn't asking for a commitment is comforting. The fact that this is Logan—the guy who holds my first for every important moment in life, the guy who has held my heart since high school—makes my decision easy.

"Okay," I answer, not considering that he's also the guy who could destroy me. His lips are on mine before I can say anything else. Just one night, that's all I need, too.

JUST ONE NIGHT
CHAPTER TWO

One year later …

Sara

My back rubs against the tree, and when Logan pushes his body against mine, the bark digs into my skin. In this moment, I don't care. I will accept it. I'll even enjoy it. There's zero amount of pain that could keep me from kissing Logan Parker.

The fear of what comes after kissing Logan, is different.

There are only three things in life that terrify me. The first is dying from a freak accident—shark attack, tripping and cracking my head open, or choking while I'm alone come to mind. The second is not being successful. I took college classes in high school and doubled my course load once I was actually attending the local campus just so I could be ahead in my career. My father raised me well, and letting all of that go to waste is a scary thought. And the last thing that scares me, the thing that could ruin me, is committing to someone who will leave me with a broken heart. Committing to Logan Parker to be exact.

The last part was the reason I decided to travel to all the fifty states and to Europe last year. It was a last minute decision, but one night with Logan had me rethinking the two things in life I thought I knew for sure—my choice in career and rekindling a relationship with him. It was like everything I'd worked for the past few years didn't matter anymore and I was about to make a huge commitment with Logan instead of my career. I thought getting away, far away, would make us both forget what it feels like to be together.

Clearly, I was wrong.

I run my hands through his hair and pull him closer. I love the way his body feels against mine. I dreamed of this moment almost every day that I was away.

His lips trail soft and tender kisses from just below my ear down to my chest. Another moan slips past my lips from his touch. The noises I make when I'm with him are uncontrollable. Fighting it has always been pointless from day one.

Logan pulls away, leaving his hands to rest on my hips. He locks a dreamy gaze with mine and my heart starts to race, the way it does every time his eyes are on me. It makes me feel wanted, desired. I imagine I give him the same exact look.

It doesn't help that he's wearing a pair of khaki slacks with a pressed, white, button-down shirt today. Or that his blonde hair is cut short and shining lighter from the heat of the sun, or that no matter where we are, he keeps those bright blue eyes that sparkle focused on me. The fact I know he has an amazing and almost unbelievably firm body underneath all those clothes really tests the control I have over how much I want him right now.

His pleased grin reveals straight, white teeth.

"I don't think we should sneak around anymore, Sara," Logan whispers, moving his hand to mine and pulling me into his arms.

Since I've been back from Europe, sneaking around has been our thing. I left with the idea I wanted space, but I returned with the idea I need Logan. I even had a weak moment and came home to see him for a few days.

Our group of friends; Kelsey, Beth, Logan, Ethan, and myself are close, and I don't want to ruin that, so telling anyone we've started something new isn't at the top of my list. It's been nothing but a few stolen, secret moments together. Moments we never talk about to anyone but each other, not even with Kelsey, my best friend. And I want to tell her so bad.

A part of me likes the idea of sneaking around. It makes everything between us more electrifying. Not knowing what will happen, not planning anything out, just going with whatever emotion I have right then and there makes me feel free. It's the total opposite of everything in my life. Plus, the feeling of being caught gives me such a rush.

Especially right now. We're at my father's house for my twenty-third birthday, and we're hiding in the trees on the side of the house. It's a beautiful, sunny June day and everyone is in the backyard enjoying the barbeque he throws for me each year. Still, anyone could turn the corner and find us.

I love it.

"Sara? Did you hear what I said?" Logan asks, rubbing my arms and hooking his gaze on mine.

"Yes, I did. I'm sorry. I was completely zoning out."

"I could see that." He chuckles.

"If you don't want to sneak around, what do you want?" I ask, mentally crossing my fingers he still wants what he wanted before I left. Me.

His smirk gives me my answer.

"I'm pretty sure you already know."

My heart begins beating faster as I control my body from jumping up and down, or more specifically, onto him. My lack of outward excitement doesn't come off positively. Logan's watching me with a worried expression.

"I know you're scared, but I think it's time we make this official," he says with a hopeful grin. "I was an idiot to let you leave last year without at least asking you to stay. What I want in life isn't going to just fall into my hands. I have to work for it, and working for an 'us' is what I want."

"Okay," I answer.

Logan grips my shoulders and pushes me away at arm's length. He looks me in the eye and a smile I've never seen but love already stretches across his face.

"Okay? As in, okay we're officially a couple?"

"Yep."

My back hits the tree fast and his lips press against mine. I'm not sure if I'm seeing stars because my head hit the trunk or because he's kissing me like I'm his air and he can finally breathe. *He's never kissed me like this before.* His hands start exploring every part of my body, leaving a tingling trail everywhere they touch. A giddy feeling rushes to my core as Logan grips my ass, lifting me until my legs are wrapped around him. With his hands cupping my butt, he holds me there, pressing me against his hips as they grind into mine.

What else has he been holding back?

He breaks away quickly, breathing hard and lowering my feet back to the ground. Before I can tell him I want to keep going, he grabs my hand.

"Come on. We better go before your dad finds me and kills me for sneaking around with you."

I nod and step past him, laughing as he tickles my sides from behind me. I know happiness is written all over my face. This is it. This is the moment I take a risk and begin to conquer one of my biggest fears.

Logan

The sound of Sara's laughter is the most incredible noise I've ever heard. I don't care how whipped I sound when I say it or even think it. I'm lucky as hell she's giving me a second chance. Between my last year of college coming up, a student loan that I'm falling behind on paying, a rent check two months past due, and a sister I've been trying to contact but have heard nothing from, luck is something I haven't had in a while.

I pull Sara back at the waist until she's walking next me. Never letting my hand leave her side, I sneak a glimpse to admire her. Her blonde hair is braided to the side. Her peach summer dress falls just above her knees and flows with each step she takes. The color makes her tan look darker. She isn't wearing any jewelry or shoes, which is odd because this girl loves her accessories.

I watch as a glowing smile never leaves her lips. She squeezes the hand that's tangled with mine as she looks up to me with her light blue eyes. I'm not just quoting a line when I say that she has the most beautiful and breathtaking eyes I have ever seen. They are eyes that twist and break any control I have.

Sara's father's house is at the base of Wind Valley's mountain and is surrounded by tall oak trees, giving it a slight forest look. Her smiling continues as we step past the last tree. I squeeze her tiny figure again as she walks in front of me. At my touch she trips, falling into my shoulder. I turn her upright, facing me. Right then, she does something amazing. She stands on the tips of her toes and presses a gentle kiss to my lips right in front of everyone we know.

Expecting to hear shouts and hollers, we hear nothing. Glancing to the party, I see why. Not a single person is looking our way. Sara's happy smile is still glued in place.

"And all this time we always thought someone would catch us, when really, no one was ever looking," she says, sounding as shocked as I am. We laugh as we join the party.

"Did you know Kelsey and Ethan eloped last month?" I ask, taking a seat at the eight-person metal rectangle patio set. Sara sits on my left knee, resting against me as I wrap my arms around her.

"I might have known that." She smirks, leaning forward to open the closest cooler to us. I never let my hands stray from somehow touching her. She hands me a beer and grabs a Pepsi for herself, flipping the top and taking a drink. It's always amazed me that she practically owns a bar, yet she hardly drinks alcohol. I think I've seen her drink three times in all the years I've known her. "You do know Kelsey is my best friend, right? We don't really keep secrets from each other."

She's lying. She never told Kelsey about last summer. I

would have received some sort of ass chewing from Kelsey if she had. I smile, cocking an eyebrow at her.

"Okay, so there are *some* things we don't share." She laughs.

"Yeah, I thought so," I say, giving her sides another squeeze as she squeals. It feels so good to show her how much I care for her to all our friends.

"So, does this mean you're finally out in the open with all this?" Kelsey says, sitting across from us. Ethan takes the seat next to her with a shit-eating grin on his face, too.

"What do you mean, *finally*?" Sara asks.

"Like we didn't know." Ethan laughs.

"Everyone knew something was going on," Kelsey adds. "We just didn't know what exactly that was."

With her mouth open, Sara looks over her shoulder at me.

"I never said anything"—I raise my hands in surrender form—"swear it."

She rolls her eyes but smiles at the same time.

"Yes, it does," Sara answers at the same time I nod in Ethan's direction.

"It's about freaking time," Ethan says, winking at both of us. "The tension between you two was getting a bit ridiculous."

"Shut up, it was not." Sara laughs.

"Oh it most definitely—"

"If I could please have everyone's attention!"

Sara jumps at the sound of her father's booming voice. He steps through the French doors that lead from his kitchen onto the patio and comes to a stop once he's next to us. Sara stands slowly and I do the same, holding her hand tightly in mine.

"As you all know, I have been working to expand my

business for some time now. It may just be a bar to most of you, but to me it's how I provide for myself and for my daughter, and it brings me such joy to share with all of you today the birthday gift I have for Sara."

I can feel Sara's hand stiffen so I hold on tighter. Her father turns to face us and the excitement falls from his face when he notices my arms wrapped around her. He swallows and looks me in the eye for a brief moment before returning his focus back to Sara.

"Congratulations, dear. We got the place in Colorado, and it's all yours."

Fuck. Maybe luck isn't on my side after all.

Finish reading Just One Night today!

Want more from Jami?
Subscribe to her mailing list for exclusive bonus epilogues and all the book news!

MORE BOOKS BY JAMI ROGERS

The Black Alcove Series

Just One Kiss

Just One Night

Just One Touch

Just One Moment

Just One Spark

Just One Love

The Kiss Me Crazy Series

Kiss Me Crazy

Love is Crazy

I Want Crazy

The Evergreen Brothers Series

A Boyfriend by Christmas

The Summer Wedding Hoax

A Match by Christmas

The Lust or Bust Series

The Write One

Write About You

The Write Choice

Write That Down

More Than Write

Always Been Write

Standalone Novels

Love Money

Date in the Dark (A New Years Eve Novella)

ACKNOWLEDGMENTS

I want to thank everyone who has supported me on this new journey. You've all been there for me in ways I will never be able to repay you.

It's hard to believe that this story is actually out in the world for everyone to read. I've spent a lot of time working on it, and I'm beyond happy to finally share it.

Holly, Mom, and Dad—I love you. You are the best family a girl could ask for. Every phase of writing a book is stressful, and none of you ever stopped believing in me.

Dana Volney—You listened to me day after day. You let me vent to you when I was stressed. You motivated me when I felt lost. You read my work and you never gave up on me. Thank you for being a truly amazing friend.

Mary Billiter—The day I stepped into your class was the best decision I've ever made. You taught me everything and more. Without you and your support, I would not be reaching my goals. You are an amazing person who I am honored to call my friend.

To the ladies in my Wednesday night writing class—you all rock! Your feedback and advice has been wonderful, and I will never forget any of you. See you soon.

Mallori Roth and Shira Ferwerda—Thank you for being

my beta readers on this novel and for helping me make this book stronger. You're awesome.

Grant Rogers—I can't thank you enough for being in my life. You understand how much this means to me, and your support never goes unnoticed.

Julie Sturgeon—Holy freaking amazing editing. You took the stress off and wanted nothing more than to help me develop this story into something I could be proud of. You did it and I couldn't be more thankful.

Allison Linhart, Alyssa Williamson, Kate Maxwell, Megan Phillips, and Trisha Butcher—Thank you for being there and for letting me go on and on about the books I write and the books I read. I love that you all have taken such an interest in this part of my life and I love having you to share these moments with.

And finally, thank you to the readers, bloggers, and social media fans that have read *Just One Kiss* and are spreading the word. Your support is the best thing I could ask for.

ABOUT THE AUTHOR

My name is Jami Rogers and I write new adult contemporary and adult contemporary romance novels. I *love* love and want to share my passion for happily ever afters with the world.

I was born in Wyoming and still live in the cowboy state with my husband, daughter, and two dogs. I like to read, write, run, watch movies/TV and spend time with my family. I'm horrible at returning phone calls and prefer to text, but still struggle to hit the little blue arrow to send a message once I'm finished typing my reply. My husband does 90% of the cooking in our house. Not because I'm busy – I'm just simply a bad cook.

Keep up with Jami by visiting her website www.
authorjamirogers.com
or
Subscribe to her mailing list for exclusive bonus epilogues
and all the book news!

facebook.com/AuthorJamiRogers

goodreads.com/jamirogers

bookbub.com/profile/jami-rogers

tiktok.com/@authorjamirogers